Divided Heart

Sheryl Marcoux

Divided Heart
COPYRIGHT 2018 by Sheryl Marcoux

Contact Information: titleadmin@pelicanbookgroup.com

Scripture quotations, unless otherwise indicated are taken from the King James translation, public domain.

Cover Art by *Nicola Martinez*

White Rose Publishing, a division of Pelican Ventures, LLC
www.pelicanbookgroup.com PO Box 1738 *Aztec, NM * 87410

White Rose Publishing Circle and Rosebud logo is a trademark of Pelican Ventures, LLC

Publishing History
First White Rose Edition, 2018
Paperback Edition ISBN 978-1-5223-0082-3
Electronic Edition ISBN 978-1-5223-0080-9
Published in the United States of America

1

"You can have it. You can have it all."

"Ain't no question whether we can have it or not, Beaufort. Question is, do we want you to live after we got it?"

Nate Powell crouched behind a rock and watched. He'd just traveled two thousand miles, the last thirty on foot, with one purpose in mind, and getting involved in stopping a holdup wasn't it.

It was getting dark, he was tired, and the chill of a Texan spring night would soon set in. He'd seen a campfire from afar and hoped for nothing more than to share it, but he'd approached to find firelight flickering across the nervous face of one man holding up his hands and the back of another holding up a gun.

Tin clanged as two men, pretty as a pair of skunk pigs, scavenged through Beaufort's belongings. One of them threw down a sack. "Ain't nothing here worth stealing."

That was no surprise. Judging by Beaufort's scraggly beard and even scragglier clothes, Nate could have told them the man was too poor to rob and saved them the trouble.

"Help yourself to some food," Beaufort stammered. "Jackrabbit should be about done."

One of them tore off more than his share of meat. "I don't like the way Beaufort here's looking at me. I say we kill him."

Nice way to thank the man for his hospitality. Nate hoped they were only harassing Beaufort.

"You don't like the way anyone looks at you, Mel."

"I don't like the way you look at me neither, Bill. So how about I kill you right after I kill him."

Nate bit his lip. He'd seen those names before.

"Why don't we just introduce ourselves to him proper so we can be sure he knows who we all are?" The man who said those words was the one holding the gun on Beaufort. He turned into the light and confirmed Nate's suspicions.

Nate ducked and centered himself behind the rock. Those were the names and faces on the "Wanted Dead or Alive" posters he'd been following from Kansas City to Dodge City. He didn't know anything else about the Krugar Gang other than the members were worth one thousand dollars each.

Which meant they were killers.

Nate slid his gun out of its holster then slid it back in. *I can't get involved.* Although he should have slipped away, he peered around the rock, looking for a solution for Beaufort.

"What do you say?" the man holding the gun said to the shadows. As Nate recalled, his name was Tom Drown. "Do we kill him?"

A fourth figure came into view but stayed away from the light. It was a smaller figure, and although the poster listed the name of the gang's leader as Joe Krugar, it didn't show a picture. Krugar remained elusive even now by staying in the shadows.

The figure gave a nod.

A bang pierced the quiet.

"Let him go. He's not doing you any harm," Nate

called out from behind the rock. Seemed he'd gotten himself involved, since it was his gun that had gone off.

Thumps and rustling followed as the gang scurried for cover. Snorting and shuffling of horses told where that cover was.

"Come on out." Tom was the spokesman for the gang. "Let's talk about this."

"Sure." Nate snickered. "You come out first." He couldn't resist a stupid answer to a stupider statement. He listened for the snap of a twig of an outlaw trying to flank him. Not a sound. Being in the dark and having a rock to hide behind put him in a better spot than Beaufort, who should have taken the opportunity to dive for cover.

The man had the virtue of hospitality, but quick thinking wasn't his strong suit. He started to run.

"Don't move," Tom shouted, stopping him short.

Beaufort raised his hands again.

"Beaufort here a friend of yours?" Tom called out.

"Never seen him before," Nate answered.

"Then you should have left this one alone," Tom said.

He was likely right.

"Why don't we all just leave this one alone?" Nate said. "You continue on your way, Beaufort will continue on his, and I'll continue on mine like nothing happened."

"We got to shoot Beaufort," Mel said. "He seen us."

"Well so did the one out yonder," Bill replied.

"And so did hundreds of other people passing through Kansas." Nate called out to the squatting shapes the slender silhouettes of acacia tree trunks couldn't hide.

"He knows who we are," Mel said.

"I do," Nate said. "But Beaufort here doesn't, do you, Beaufort?"

"He's right." Beaufort stood shabby and jittery, hands up, in the firelight. "I don't know who you be."

"How good a shot are you, mister?" Tom called to Nate.

"The truth?" Nate said. "Fair. But I'm good enough to get at least one of you before you figure out where I am. So who's going to make the sacrifice?"

"Bill," Tom said, "you go on over there."

A figure started to move in the wrong direction. They had no idea where Nate was hiding.

"Bill," Nate called, "sounds like you're the one they can do without."

"I ain't going out there."

Nate grinned.

"We'll wait you out until morning," Tom said. "We ain't in no hurry."

Nate leaned against the rock. He was no gunman. In the daylight he'd have no chance at all. He peered behind, into a darkness that once more beckoned him to escape. He'd come all this way to accomplish something long overdue, not wind up dead.

But the ragged man standing with hands raised looked like the loneliest man Nate had ever seen. Nate raked his hand through his hair. Since he couldn't outgun the gang, he'd have to outsmart them. "It's a good thing you're not in a hurry," Nate called, "because you'll have to get wherever you're going on foot."

Tom asked, "What do you mean?"

"I'm going to shoot your horses."

"Let's get out of here while we still got horses," Bill said.

Nate liked the sound of that. "I'd say we've got a standoff."

"We do," Tom said. Then he fired.

Beaufort dropped.

Nate shot a few rounds to scare the gang away from Beaufort. They fired back, but nowhere near him.

"Don't waste your bullets. We ain't going to find him tonight," Tom said. Then he called out to Nate, "Not tonight, mister, but we'll be back for you." The pounding of horse hooves followed, and they were gone.

Nate crept up to where Beaufort lay on his stomach, outside the light from the fire. He rolled him over.

Beaufort blinked.

Nate's heart almost came out of his chest. "I thought you were dead."

"I was watching his hand. When it moved toward me, I sort of fell. Bullet went through my arm." Blood had stained the ragged sleeve red.

"Well, even though they didn't kill you, that gang is nothing but a band of cold-blooded murderers." Nate heaved a sigh. "The Krugar Gang won't be looking for us tonight. We'd better forego that warm fire and a good night's rest and get you to a doctor."

Beaufort didn't argue as Nate bound up Beaufort's arm as best he could with the man's neckerchief.

Nate grabbed two sticks from the ground to use for walking. He gave one to Beaufort. Night was a treacherous time to walk, but fortunately, the moon was full and bright. Nate looked up at it as if he were seeing it for the first time. "It's been a long time since

I've been in these parts," he said as they started walking.

Beaufort plodded behind him, leaning heavily on his own stick. "Where we headed?"

Nate stared out toward Ramsden, Texas. "To the last place on earth I want to go."

"Then why would you want to go there?"

"A woman." Nate stepped wide around the shadowy shape of a cholla cactus. "Last I'd heard, she hadn't married. But even if that's still the case, it's a thousand to one shot she'd give me the time of day after what I'd done to her." But he'd come a long way from the unruly youth who'd left his hometown years ago. A *long* way.

"She must be one special gal."

The sign by the picket fence indicated that the doctor was still where he used to be. Nate handed Beaufort enough money to pay the doctor, get a few good meals, and stay in the hotel if he needed. After several knocks, a light lit up a window. Nate slipped away into the night, not wanting to be seen by anyone.

Then he quickened his pace toward the direction his heart drove him, but common sense rebuked was a waste of time.

~*~

Who's knocking at the door at this hour?

Hattie Brown leaped out of bed and snatched the shotgun. The moonlight poured through the window and lit her house well enough to see. *That knocking better be an emergency. If it isn't*—she cocked back the hammer—*it will be.* The knocking came from the front door, so she headed toward the window where she'd be able to get a look.

Rap, rap, rap.

It was a quiet, patient knock. She'd have even described it as polite—had it not been for the impolite hour.

If this was an emergency, whoever it was should have said so. Which suggested the visitor was just seeing if anyone inside was awake, because he was fixing to rob the place.

Good luck finding something worth stealing. She had some crockery, four sacks of flour, and a cook stove about as easy to move as a mule with its hooves nailed to the floorboards. But what little she had was valuable to her, and she aimed to protect it.

With a fingertip, she separated the curtains just wide enough to peer outside. The moon was bright enough, but she couldn't see the intruder from this angle. She had to try another. Like the angle she'd get from sneaking up from behind.

She eased the window open. It gave a few inches and then wouldn't budge. "You sure you want to have a go of it with me?" she whispered to the window. If one way to trap a rabbit didn't work, sure as shooting there was another way. She looked around for that other way and found it involved the sledgehammer she kept in the kitchen. There was a reason folks called her hard-as-nails Hattie Brown. Nothing stood between her and what she'd set her mind to do.

She tapped the bottom of the window with the sledgehammer. Yesterday's rain had swelled the wood so that it still wouldn't budge. She gave it one good whack, which was more than it needed, and the window slammed against the top of its casing.

Had the intruder heard? Must have.

Shotgun in hand, she crawled out the window and slipped around the house. Then, she spotted a man at her door.

She looked at the henhouse and woodshed for evidence of anyone else. The hens weren't putting up a ruckus, and the rooster who watched over them wasn't in an uproar. So it was likely just the one man. She made her way wide to take him by surprise. But instead, he took her by surprise.

"Hello, Hattie."

She stumbled back. Either her ears were playing tricks on her or her heart was the culprit. *It can't be him.* She raised her shotgun. "Who're you?"

He stepped away from the shadows of the house, and moonlight lit up the once-familiar features of a man's face.

This has to be a dream. Just in case her eyes and ears were playing tricks, she demanded, "What do you want?"

A voice that had always made her weak for him answered. "You, Hattie. I came back for you."

2

The sight of Hattie in a long white nightdress, barefoot, and bathed in moonlight was worth every minute of Nate's journey, and then some. Every rumbling hour on the train. Every bumpy mile on the stagecoach. Every throbbing blister on his feet from walking the rest of the way so he wouldn't be seen. She was as beautiful as he remembered her, and that she'd come out alone and carrying a shotgun suggested she had no husband.

The moon's glow illuminated her olive skin and the ebony braid that poured over one shoulder and down toward her waist. But her exotic black eyes—a man could never forget a gaze from them once they'd connected with his own.

She cocked her head as if to say, *"Where've you been, Nate?"*

He answered. Partially. "I've established a comfortable life back East."

Still no response. Rightly so.

"You're one of a kind, Hattie, a special kind. I realize that now, and I'm ready to do right by you." How could he describe his long struggle to come back? If only he could take out his heart and put it into her chest so she could feel how much he ached for her. "I love you, Hattie."

~*~

I love you.

The words echoed in her head like a recurring dream. Those were the last words Nate Powell would have uttered to her, but the ones she'd always longed to hear him say. If he was a dream, why was she talking to an apparition, aiming her shotgun at it, and hoping…? Hoping that it was all real.

Could this really be his ever-so-serious face, even more handsome with manhood? Were these the unruly yellow curls of his youth calmed with maturity into short blond waves? And the voice—even, soft-spoken, intelligent—wasn't this the voice she'd yearned to hear again?

The emptiness awakened. It was a place where being half white had left her feeling different from everyone else and where working as a saloon girl left her shunned and lonely. Neither ever mattered to Nate, and being in his company was the closest thing she'd ever felt to being loved.

She thought she'd gotten over him long ago, but the tenderness she'd once had for him stampeded back over her heart.

That's how she knew he was real. The years hadn't diminished her love for him one bit, only buried them under a heap of hurt. Seeing him again caused those yearnings to dig their way out of the pain he'd left her in. Just when she'd started to get a foothold on things.

Her face heated. *How dare he come back and say those words to me now.* "You've been gone seven years. If you want me to even entertain the notion of allowing you to court me, you'd better have a good explanation for being gone *that* long."

~*~

Nate had a good explanation, just one he couldn't tell her, so he simply answered, "That's how long it took."

"How long *what* took? You only had one year left of schooling, and with a mind like yours..."

A mind like his. She didn't know the half of it. The half she did know was the obvious part. When they were schoolchildren, he was the top student who tutored the rest. So Hattie was correct in assuming he'd finished his last year of college in the customary time. He'd graduated *summa cum laude*, in fact. It was the other half of his mind which had kept him away so long. He read an accusation in her narrowing eyes. "No, I haven't been with another woman."

She leaned forward. "Then explain it to me, Nate. Explain to me why you've been away so long. Explain to me why you never even wrote me one single letter. Explain to me why you never so much as said good-bye. And explain to me why you come to my house in the middle of the night, sneaking around like a fox outside a henhouse."

He stared at her. Had he expected her to take all this in faith? What a heart-driven fool he was. "I didn't want anyone else to know I was here. Just you. As for my absence—" Should he explain it? No, because he'd never be able to face her again. "I was—establishing myself."

Fibers of wool bristled in her satin voice. "With whom?"

Her accusation wounded him. "I deserve that. But you're wrong."

"No, Nate, you deserve a whole lot worse. But if

I'm wrong, set me straight." Her eyes softened, pleaded.

His chest ached to tell her the truth. He owed it to her. But the truth came at too high a price. "You're all I want here. That's why I sneaked in."

"And you think that's all there is to it?"

"What do you mean 'that's all there is to it?' Isn't love reason enough? I thought you loved me. I thought your love was strong as steel. Did seven years rust it away? Because it only welded mine for you into place. I know now, Hattie. I *know* that I love you."

She stared at him with an unconvinced expression.

He tossed a hand toward her house. "Look around you, for Pete's sake. You deserve better than a lousy life in this old shack, and I can give it to you."

She cocked her head. "Give what to me?"

"I'll buy you a castle. I'll make you the queen you really are. There's a comfortable life waiting for us in Massachusetts, and I don't want to spend another day living it without you. Just tell me that you love me, Hattie," he pleaded. "It's that simple."

"That simple, huh? Everything comes easy for you, doesn't it? Good looks, intelligence, money. You got everything it takes." Her glare settled on his fine jacket. "And then some."

He somberly stared back at her. "If I have everything it takes, then why is it so difficult for you to say that you love me?"

~*~

Difficult? Hattie snorted when she wanted to cry. If only he knew how difficult it was not to run into his arms and say those words over again. Heartbreak.

12

That's all he'd ever given to her. "You have no idea what it took for me to establish my 'lousy life' in this 'old shack.' You can't imagine what it took me to make friends. Friends who've become family to me. Family I can *trust*. Which is a lot more than I can say about you."

The thrill of seeing him wore off, and the chill of the night air ruffling her nightdress set in.

The weight of the shotgun in her hands had become burdensome.

"You've had more than enough chances with me, Nate. There's no more making amends. Even if those amends involve placing a jewel-studded crown on my head, because loving you hurts too much. Besides—" if he cared for her half as much as she'd cared for him, then what she was about to say would strike him back one well-deserved blow and give him a good reason never to return. "I've got a beau." She raised the barrel of the shotgun to add persuasion to her words. "I've gone on with my life. Now get out and get on with yours."

~*~

Hattie's statement hit Nate harder than a spray of buckshot. It was by no means unbelievable. But it was devastating.

"What's the matter?" she said.

Maybe he'd hesitated too long.

"You think I lost what it takes to light a spark in a man's eye?"

From what he saw in front of him, he could attest that at twenty-nine years old, Hattie still had more than her fair share of what it took to set a man's heart on fire. He couldn't help but ask. "Who is he?"

"The Reverend."

"The *Reverend*?"

She inaccurately read into his look of stupor. "You think it's so surprising that a preacher would be interested in me?"

"It's *you* being interested in a preacher that stumps me." Any man could be weakened by those black, temptress eyes.

"I've gotten religion, Nate."

He was speechless. That was the last thing he expected to hear, but at least it explained her interest in a preacher. "Does he know about your past?"

"You mean—the Reverend you hired on to marry you to Lillian?"

A blow for a blow. He shouldn't have said that. But he'd thought of this night for so long, and to lose her to...*religion*?

"You going to tell him about me?"

And ruin any chance of her being happy? "No, Hattie, I'm not."

"Then what *are* you going to do?"

Worse than facing the barrel of her shotgun was facing the anger flaring in her eyes. Anger with his name on it. She didn't want him anymore, and a woman like Hattie could have any man she wanted. Even a preacher.

He succumbed to what he so well deserved. "I wish you happiness."

He soaked in his last sight of her alluring eyes and the way the breeze brushed her nightdress against her slender form. Then he forced himself to turn away from her and accept the regret he'd have to live with for the rest of his life.

He would return to Massachusetts to an expensive house that was nothing more to him than a place where he slept and kept his belongings. It would never be a home without a wife, and Hattie was the only woman for him. The years spent without her had been the loneliest of his life. The darkness ahead filled the emptiness inside him, and he stared into it. He'd known from the start that his chances of her still loving him were a long shot. Like having a hundred coins on one side of a scale and only one on the other—and expecting that one coin could somehow tip the scale in his favor. Hope had made that one shiny coin seem a lot bigger than it was.

But the truth was that trust was as fragile as a porcelain vase. Once shattered, it could never be repaired.

3

"We could both get this over and done with if you'd lie still long enough so I can kill you."

That would have made the task easier on both of them if the chicken was willing to comply with what Hattie had in mind. But instead the chicken put up a ruckus, squabbling and kicking at her with sharp claws as she held it down to the chopping block. It slashed her arm, and blood poured out.

This one's a fighter.

They were all fighters. It was Hattie who dodged those claws better on some days than others. The proof was on her forearms. They were cut up, healed over, and then cut up again. Life was full of fresh and reopened wounds from making a living.

And from just plain living.

No, she wouldn't think about Nate. And she wouldn't think about finding an easier chicken to kill either, because Hattie was also a fighter.

And she had an axe.

The toughest chickens have the most tender meat, she'd convinced herself. Well, the philosophy sounded good, anyway.

The axe came down swiftly and mercifully. Too bad love wasn't as kind on the heart.

She strung up the chicken and went inside to tend to her injury. It seemed Hattie had more of her own blood on her apron than the chicken's. It reminded her of how being in love with Nate had been. There was always a struggle, and she always ended with more wounds than he did.

The gash on her forearm was long and deep. It could use some stitching up, but she just tied a clean rag around it. She made chicken pies for a living and had to get a dozen of them to Kate's Eatery by nine each morning.

One chicken was all it took to fill the order. One fighting, squabbling, slashing chicken that she'd have to pluck, boil, and debone. The rest was just flour, water, shortening, vegetables, and a mess to clean up after. But it was nowhere as bad as the mess she had yet to clean up after seeing Nate.

Why did he have to come back, Lord? He always left me in a muddle of hurt and yearning for him, and he's done it again. Please get him out of my heart. I don't want to love him anymore. Even though she'd told Nate to go away, her feelings for him hadn't left with him. It seemed she'd fallen hopelessly in love with a man who was no good for her, and she couldn't climb out of that love.

Hattie headed into town to deliver the pies in a wagon drawn by an old, rickety mare that looked the way Hattie felt. She stopped at Doc's along the way and found him outside.

"How's that wife of yours doing?" Hattie called out.

"She's still under the weather," Doc said. "It seems I can treat everything but the common cold."

Or an aching heart. "I got just the cure." Hattie handed him a jar of chicken soup she'd made that morning.

"I appreciate it." Doc noticed the blood-stained rag. "Your arm looks like it could use some attention."

"I'll be all right," she said. Her arm, anyway.

She continued downtown where the businesses were opening and the sun was warming up the air. People strolling along the boardwalks moved as slowly as Hattie's horse. As Hattie's heart.

She spotted Brawley, a friend's husband, on the walk. Brawley and Aggie had four small children and a farm to tend to, so neither came to town often. Since Aggie had the upper hand in their relationship, Hattie couldn't resist teasing him. "Did Aggie let you out, or did you escape?"

"She don't know I'm gone. I sneaked off to buy something for her birthday. Hey. Got any idea what a lady would like?"

Hattie thought on that for a moment. Right off, she knew the answer he was looking for, but it was the way he'd worded the question that slowed her down. Did a woman start turning into "just one of the fellows" if she was still unmarried and closer to thirty than she was eighteen?

"Buy her some ribbons," Hattie said. "Blue would look nice on her."

"Hello, Hattie." Clayton, the telegrapher, spotted her as he unlocked the door to his office. "Give me a minute, and I'll lend you a hand." He knew her routine and always helped her unload.

There was someone else who knew her routine. For some reason, Hattie still referred to him as Boss, probably because she'd worked for him for so long. Everyone else had absorbed her as part of the town, but Boss wanted to absorb her back into his saloon where he'd worked her like a slave and beat her like a dog. He stood in front of his saloon at this hour every morning and glared her down for quitting on him.

"Got something you want to say to Hattie?" a deep voice called out to Boss.

Boss swung his glance over to Zachariah Keane and then went inside. No one argued with Zachariah.

"Let me give you a hand with those, Hattie." Zachariah grinned toward the telegraph office. "Can't trust Clayton with your pies. He's apt to take one."

"I can't trust you with them either," she said. "You're apt to take two."

"You've got to sympathize with me." Zachariah put on his pity-me face. "You know the way my wife cooks."

Poor Zachariah. Lillian was so naive about preparing food that when they first married, she thought peppercorns were dried currants, and so she'd fed him peppercorn muffins, peppercorn waffles, peppercorn griddle cakes.... "I tried to teach her, Zachariah. Honest I did. Cooking just isn't her gift." That was an understatement. Lillian was beautiful, she had a fancy English accent, and she had a sweet disposition. Hattie reckoned Lillian's lack of cooking skills was God's way of reminding Zachariah he hadn't gone to Heaven yet.

"Then you know who your best customer is." Zachariah snatched up two pies like he was deciding which one he was going to have for lunch. It seemed Kate's Eatery kept him from starving.

Hattie smiled as he carried the pies inside the eatery. Aside from him being one of her most loyal customers, Zachariah and his wife were also her best friends. Her smile faded, because they were also friends who'd had a bad run in with Nate way back when. She didn't want to talk about it but figured she'd better tell Zachariah about the visit.

"Nate came around last night," she said.

Zachariah was heading back to the wagon to fetch more pies when her statement fastened his boots to the walk. Judging by the look of shock in his eyes, it was a good thing his hands were empty. His boots were still stuck, but at least he managed to loosen his tongue. "Nate? You sure it was him?"

"Do you think I don't know what Nate looks like?" Or how it felt to see him again.

"After all this time?" A look of concern crossed his face. "Care to tell me what he wanted?"

"He wanted me to go back East with him."

Zachariah knew how infatuated she'd once been with Nate and that he was no good for her. "And?"

"And I told him 'no' and he left and that's all there is to it. So there's no use stirring up Lillian and getting her upset. He's gone." Those last two words choked out hard.

A pause from Zachariah suggested he wasn't convinced. "You really think he's gone for good?"

It was too hard to outright say yes. "Would you come around again if someone held a shotgun to you?"

He responded with a lingering look she didn't understand. It seemed Zachariah could read everyone, but no one could read him. Did he know something about Nate she didn't know?

Zachariah set himself into motion again and picked up more pies but with less enthusiasm than before. "How are you doing, Hattie?" He knew she was aching for Nate. She couldn't pull the cowhide over Zachariah's eyes.

"I'm doing." The gashes on her arms didn't compare with the blow of seeing Nate again. Her heart stumbled, but she was determined to regain her footing and stay on course. Though she wanted to feel the caress of his arms around her shoulders once again, she had to listen to her head and not her heart.

4

Nate had spent the night camped out in a ravine in the company of a few pesky mosquitoes and a dying mesquite. Though he'd left Hattie's sight, he couldn't leave her altogether. The next morning, he returned to spy on her to ensure she'd be all right after he left. He didn't like what he saw. Her life was as tough and jagged as the serrated blades of the yacca he hid behind.

Eyes cast down, she walked with a forced gait from her ramshackle house to the henhouse. His heart ached seeing her in the rags she wore, a faded calico dress that fit her poorly, and a stained apron. *You should be wearing satin, not only because of how beautiful you are, but because of who you are.*

She'd always held herself with quiet dignity despite the scorn she'd received. While women had looked down on her for working in a saloon, he'd always looked up to her for courage in the way she stood up to the men.

You're royalty, Hattie, royalty that fate misplaced.

A limp chicken dangled in her hand as she trudged back to her shack. Behind the window, she peeled potatoes, and then swept sweat from her unsmiling face, smearing her forehead with flour. She looked beaten.

You deserve better than this. If you'd only give me another chance.

The college degree he'd earned and his reputation for excellence had won him a job as the youngest vice president of the Massachusetts National Bank. He made enough money to buy her everything she could want. He shook his head at the weathered planks. Happiness had always eluded her, and he was especially guilty of keeping it away from her. Something had blinded him from seeing her worth. Some*one*.

Zachariah Keene.

Nate's hand balled into a fist of its own accord. "Enemy" was too mild a word to describe the man behind the reason Nate had left Ramsden and why he couldn't be seen now. Nate's fist trembled with desire to… No, he couldn't let Zachariah get to him. He'd be out of Ramsden soon enough. *I just need to know Hattie will be all right, and then I'm on my way.*

She *did* say she had a beau.

Nate never fathomed she'd land in the arms of a preacher. There must have been something special about the man to have won such an extraordinary woman. Was he the one who'd tamed her heart—or did he even know about her past? *If he really is a man of God, he shouldn't care about what she was then, only who she is now.* A church-going woman. Another thing Nate never would have expected.

He must be quite a man. Learned, dignified, and handsome enough to have snagged Hattie's interest. Hattie didn't exactly say they were engaged, but if the man had half a brain….

I got what I deserved. He was the one who'd hired the Reverend in order to have himself a respectable wedding to Lillian so many years ago. He'd placed an ad in several newspapers, *"Minister Wanted."* The

Reverend answered via telegraph, *"Just finished seminary. Am interested."* Nate hired him since there was no need to know more about the man. He'd expected the Reverend would have left long ago.

But then again, Hattie was plenty of reason to stay. Which raised another question. *Why is he still just her suitor?*

Hattie was hardworking, loyal, tender, and the old biddy dress that covered her from neck to toe couldn't hide the contours of what was underneath. What man snared in the depth of her eyes wouldn't want to entangle himself further with her in marriage?

Nate's curiosity about the Reverend crested. It also set a new course for his feet through the scrub and shin-high patches of grass. *This job interview is long overdue.* Nate quickened his pace toward the church to find some answers, when a faraway sound stopped him short.

Bang!

Who'd be out here in the middle of nowhere shooting? There was no game out here.

Two more shots.

Could it be?

Nate dove into the grass.

Was the Krugar Gang tracking him down? If it was those murdering thieves, Hattie didn't live far away.

Needing to find out where and who the gunshots came from took Nate away from the church and toward the sound of the bullets. Staying low, he scurried from bush to bush until he came to the last thing he expected to find.

The Reverend, dressed in the garments of his trade. The man was nothing like Nate had imagined.

He was tall and lanky. And second—
   Bang!
   Why was a preacher of peace shooting a gun?

5

Nate eased his way into the open. "I didn't know a preacher needed a gun."

The Reverend whirled and dropped the gun, setting off a bullet. It missed Nate's shoe and went into the wilds beyond.

"I didn't mean to—"

"Try to shoot off my foot?"

"I didn't expect anyone to be around. I suppose it would help if I were wearing these." He fished a pair of eyeglasses from his saddlebag and fumbled to put them on. By the way he squinted through the lenses, even they wouldn't help his aim.

Nate cleared his throat to cover a snicker. "What are you doing so far from the church, Reverend?"

"I didn't want to disturb anyone. I've discovered guns make a lot of noise."

A man who'd figured out guns made a lot of noise? *This* was the man who would make Hattie happy? Nate picked up the "noise maker" from the ground and handed it back to the Reverend.

That was a mistake.

The Reverend twirled the pistol around his trigger finger and dropped it again.

Nate jumped back as a bullet chipped a good chunk off the tree the Reverend's horse was tethered to. The animal snorted as though it had grown accustomed to these close brushes with death.

"I'm learning how to shoot," the Reverend said.

"From what I can tell so far," Nate said, "all you have to do is drop your gun." Nate looked at the bottles set up on barrels in the far distance. Even he couldn't hit one of them. "Your targets might be a bit too ambitious for a beginner." Frankly, only an expert could hit one of those bottles from this distance. Nate asked, "What do you plan on killing from this far away?"

"Rattlesnakes. I thought it prudent to have some means to protect myself from them."

"And you think you're going to see them from this far off?" *Especially with those eyeglasses?* "Don't you think rattlesnakes would be crawling on the ground and not flying four feet up in the air?" Nate rubbed his jaw.

Was this the same man Hattie had said was courting her? Or did someone switch preachers since she'd last seen him?

"How long have you been in Ramsden?"

"I've been here about seven years."

This was indeed Hattie's man. And he was just figuring out now that they had rattlers?

Nate found something else odd as he picked the gun out of the dirt again. This wasn't any old revolver. "You bought a Colt .44 to kill snakes?"

"Do you think it'll do the trick?"

Nate shook his head at the man's stupidity. "It's enough to kill a snake and all its relatives." *If you can hit it.* "You might be better off with a shotgun." A long-barreled weapon that fired a spray of bullets might be more practical. And if the Reverend still couldn't hit a snake with one of the bullets, maybe he could bludgeon it to death with the stock.

Nate handed the revolver back.

The man held it as though it were a hot biscuit. He was more of a danger to himself than the snakes were.

"I don't recognize you," the Reverend said as the revolver settled in his hand. He aimed for one of the bottles. His eyeglasses were in the right direction, but the barrel of the Colt was a good twenty degrees off.

"I'm Nate Powell. The man who hired you."

"Reverend Everton." The man absently offered the gun instead of just his hand for Nate to shake.

Nate raised his hands. "Hold on. I'm just passing through. Maybe you should take the bullets out and get used to the gun first."

"Oh. Yes." It seemed to take him a moment to realize he had the barrel pointed straight at Nate. "How do I...?"

Nate snatched the revolver and emptied the bullets out of the cylinders. He handed it back and then poured the handful of bullets into the man's palm.

The Reverend dropped them like a handful of red ants. "I'm afraid weapons make me nervous."

"How about women?"

"Excuse me?"

"I don't see a woman around." It was a roundabout way of inquiring about how the Reverend felt about Hattie.

"I'm afraid I'm worse with women than I am with guns."

Well, that explained why he and Hattie hadn't gotten further than courtship.

~*~

"Let's get this off you," Hattie said to her old mare

when they'd returned home.

The bandage wrapped around Hattie's arm was soaked with fresh blood from reopening the wound. She ignored the bleeding as she released Nellie from her harness, led her into the barn, and then watered her. Hattie wasn't ready to go into a lonely house yet, so she lingered in the barn. She gave the horse some oats. "You're happy being a single gal, aren't you, Nellie?"

The old horse was calm and content. Any more docile, and it would be dead.

"Do you ever think about the past? Do you ever have regrets?" She looked at a creature whose only interest was eating, but Hattie kept talking. "It seems that turning to God saves the soul, but it doesn't always save the mind from wishing you'd done things right in the first place.

"I remember a time when I wore my dresses low on the shoulder and high on the leg." Hattie started brushing the horse. "Yup, Nellie, my job was to flirt with men and keep them drinking so Boss could get their money. I was good at what I did, too. Always smiling and hating every minute of it.

"The men who came in always smelled like skunks, and I'd swear Boss would signal me to flirt with the one who stank the worst. The saloon was like a big crate I was stuck in, and I didn't think there was a world beyond the walls. At least, not a world that wanted me in it. The only pleasant thing that ever came through the door was Nate."

Nate had left Ramsden, and she'd left the saloon because she'd come to realize something about being a saloon girl. It might have been the right way to show off to a man that she was a woman, but it was the wrong way to let him know she was also a lady who wanted to feel safe and protected in his arms—and his arms alone.

Nate.

She stared off into the past where she could see him in the corner of the saloon in the same old chair watching her. She gazed out the barn door as though she might see him heading back to Massachusetts and half grinned at the fancy life she could have had.

"The Lord, Nellie. I reckoned He's what saved me from leaving with Nate." She paused a moment, lest a tear come, because she'd discovered there was a world outside the saloon that wanted her in it. "Most everyone here's become like family to me. Especially Zachariah." Her love for him ran deeper than blood. There was no person she admired more. No one who'd helped her out as much as he did.

She looked at her stained bandage. "Reckon I ought to get a fresh rag and stop aggravating this cut."

Nellie munched, oblivious to everything but the oats.

"Reckon I also ought to stop telling my troubles to a horse."

Hattie pushed the loneliness away and gave the horse a pat on the neck. "Better not die on me, Nellie, because I'll have to turn to those nasty chickens to tell my troubles to."

She went into the house to clean up the morning's baking mess. Her cookery was crusted with dried-up potato starch and the bench was still caked with flour. Overwhelmed at a chore that suddenly seemed too big to tackle, she sat down, seeing what she'd been trying not to feel inside.

The mess Nate had left behind.

It was hard to pray because her heart and her head had different petitions. *I love Nate, Lord, but he's brought me nothing but heartache. Besides, I'm not his saloon girl anymore. I'm Yours now. And I know You've got another fish for me to fry.*

The Reverend.

If she wanted a man who could help her stay on the straight and narrow, he was as devout as they came. But she hadn't done much to bait the hook on her fishing line to catch him. The folks in town who knew her secret, kept it. But the Reverend deserved to know about her past. But that wasn't as lousy as the other predicament a romance with the Reverend presented to Hattie.

Frankly, she found her one fish to fry as attractive as a flounder with eyeglasses.

6

"There's no way on this earth a woman like you can respect a man like that."

Hattie crossed her arms because Nate was right, but she wouldn't give him the satisfaction of letting him know it. "But I can respect a two-timing weasel like you?"

Once again Nate was at Hattie's door. This time he'd come at a more considerate hour. Instead of the middle of the night, he'd come just after nightfall.

Though she was still dressed, the door was closed between them. In fact, she'd made double sure it was locked, because it wasn't so much Nate she wanted to keep out. She wanted to keep herself in.

"I didn't say you should respect me."

"Then what are you saying? That you think you're better than him?"

"I didn't say anything of the sort. Stop putting words in my mouth."

Arrogance and conceit. That's what she'd wanted to hear from him. Not sensibility. "I thought you left. Why are you back?"

"Because I know you can't be in love with the Reverend. The man's a clumsy oaf. He wouldn't know what to do with a wife even if she came with instructions."

He'd hit the truth dead center.

That does it. Hattie threw open the door. She had

something to say to Nate, and he would hear it loud and clear. But the moment she saw him in the glow of her lamp, she regretted opening the door. He was so handsome and refined that she almost forgot what she meant to say. "At least I can trust him to stay out of the arms of another woman."

"That's because the Reverend couldn't aim his way to her house, let alone her arms. And you still have it fluttering around in your head that I was with another woman."

No, it wasn't "fluttering in her head," it was lodged in her heart. She should have gnawed on him for talking to her like that, but she wanted him to prove her suspicions wrong. "You want to convince me otherwise?"

Nate hesitated. "Come on, Hattie. The Reverend's as clumsy as a drunk with two left hands."

So you can't prove me wrong. He'd avoided answering what she needed to know. *I wish at least you could be honest with me, Nate.* And speaking of honesty, Nate's astute blue eyes and his smart, polished appearance were hard to ignore—especially when he was right about the Reverend. So Hattie mussed him up. "I'd rather lay my heart on the ground for the Reverend to trip over than for you to trample over. Again."

His clamped jaw ended that discussion.

Hattie wanted to end them all. "Now, I already told you I don't want you coming around. So tell me something. What will it take to get you to stop knocking on my door at night?"

"Knowledge." Coming from Nate it wasn't so odd.

"What kind of knowledge?"

"The knowledge you're happy, or at least have a

chance to be. Because I know you're not."

"And you think I'll be happy with you?"

He fell quiet again, his blue gaze drawing her in.

She blinked away and stared into the night beyond where he'd left her seven years earlier. "Let me tell you a thing or two, Mr. Nate 'Ain't You Just Rich and Wonderful' Powell. I'm a lot happier without you than I'd ever be with you. And you can take *that* back East with you."

His voice softened. "I'll give you everything, Hattie." In his solemn face, she saw the promise of a fine home, beautiful dresses, and the best a man could give. That is—until another woman came along who was just as infatuated with him as she was. She knew because he'd cheated on her once before. Cheated? Who was she fooling? He'd become downright engaged to Lillian right under Hattie's nose. So, who else did he have nibbling on his line now? "I've already had your everything. I'm better off without it. Now, as I recall, I'd told you to get out. Stay away from the Reverend, too. Don't you dare come near me or him, or I'll go straight to the sheriff." She glared him down to sear in a final statement. "Get out of my life, Nate. I don't ever want to see your face again."

His response was bittersweet. Sweet because of the long, tender look he gave her. And then bitter because of the way he quietly looked down.

Her love wasn't worth fighting for. Not like Lillian's had been. Hattie slammed the door. She leaned her back against the wooden barrier. *I want to marry a pious man, Lord.* She raised her eyes. *So I'm doing the right thing, aren't I?*

She had to admit the Reverend was a bumbler. Actually, he was worse than a blindfolded bull in a china shop, and she could never imagine him being the man she needed him to be.

Only Nate had ever caught her fancy. But it wasn't Nate's good looks that had held her in awe of him. It was how a gentleman like him once cared for a woman like her.

She shouldn't have accused him of being arrogant, because he'd never kept their relationship secret. Everyone in town knew about them. He was rich; she was poor. He was white; she was...mixed. He didn't care about any of that. He just cared about her.

That stopped the day Lillian had come to town.

Hattie hugged her shoulders, remembering what it was like being in his arms. There was something in his smile that had once steadied her. Something serious, something compassionate, something so tender it made her feel not so much as a woman who'd gone bad but as a woman who'd had things go bad.

She dropped her hands. She hoped for better days ahead with the Reverend. *I don't trust you anymore, Nate. I wish I could.* She put her hand on the door, imagining for a moment that Nate might be doing the same.

~*~

Nate stood on the other side of the door, held fast there by the yearning in his heart. *I wish I could convince you of how sorry I am, Hattie. I wish I could plead with you to trust me, to believe me. I wish I could prove to you the man I'm becoming.*

There was a time when she'd smile at him, and he wished he could go back to those days when he'd go to the saloon just to catch a glimpse of her. She'd been the most beautiful creature he'd ever seen, and she'd chosen him over every man in Ramsden.

I held everything in my arms when I held you, Hattie. Why hadn't he seen it then? If only he could go back in time, he'd hold her as if she were made of fine porcelain, because that's what her love was: a rare vase with fine, scalloped edges rimmed with gold.

And he had flung it to the ground by taking her for granted.

He held his palm to the door, wishing he could touch her one last time. He closed his eyes, imagining their hands almost touching. *If only I could reach through wood.*

So close.

Only an explanation away.

An explanation he couldn't give her.

Letting you go is the stupidest thing I've ever done. But I'd rather let you think I was with another woman and lose you to your jealous suspicions than lose you to the shame of knowing where I'd really been. Because if she thought he was with another woman, she'd simply hate him. But if she knew the truth, she'd disrespect him more than she did the bumbling Reverend.

The Reverend. Nate shook his head with regret. It was a well-deserved twist in fate that the man Nate had hired to perform his farce of a marriage to Lillian would likely wind up marrying the woman he really loved.

Craving the touch of her hand and wishing he could reach through the door, he pressed his palm against dry, splintered wood. *Are you on the other side of that door, Hattie? Do you feel the same way I do, like your chest is so crushed you can barely take your next breath?*

After the way she'd spoken to him, the answer

was probably no.

I hope you can find happiness with him, Hattie. I really do. He pulled his hand from the door.

Nate spent another night under the stars. Though his parents lived in Ramsden, in a house big enough to accommodate the U.S. Cavalry and all their relatives, and though he longed to see his mother, he'd rather sleep on a cactus than see his father again. And so, he spent much of the night staring up into the speckled black.

The next morning, he set out in the direction of the dawning sun on a journey he'd hoped he'd be taking on horseback with Hattie, with her arms around his waist and her head resting against his back. He had the money and would have sent her to rent a horse, but he couldn't risk going to town and coming across Zachariah.

Nate's trip back to Massachusetts involved a stagecoach to the train station and then a long ride back to a job where his employer had told him, *"You're good at what you do, Mr. Powell. The best I've seen, and that's why I hired you. But you're no good to me if you're not here. Two weeks. That's all I can give you."* Nate was still on track with a few days to spare, but that track began with a long walk on the outskirts of town.

Bang!

It also took him within earshot of where he'd found the Reverend practicing the day before. Apparently, the Reverend was so determined to defend himself from "flying rattlesnakes" that he'd gotten up even earlier to practice shooting.

He'd also ignored Nate's advice to get used to handling the pistol before loading it with live bullets.

Bang!

Nate shook his head. *Is the man's poor horse still alive?*

Some people just plain had no business touching a gun. Especially a Colt .44. How could Hattie have any respect for that stumblebum?

But however miniscule the pebble of appeal that drew her to the Reverend was, it was a mountain compared to what she saw in Nate.

Since he had some time to spare, maybe if he gave the Reverend some more pointers, something might sink it and earn some respectability from Hattie. Or at least spare her from getting shot in the foot by a stray bullet from a dropped gun.

Bang!

Nate walked toward the faraway sound and recognized the Reverend's horse grazing obliviously where it was tethered. *The animal must be deaf.* But at least it was still standing on four legs.

Wary of stray bullets—and of startling a man clumsy enough to shoot the one thing he wasn't aiming at—Nate circled wide and came around from behind, until he spotted the back of the man clad in black. Since it was best not to startle a jittery man, he'd wait until the Reverend needed to reload the pistol before saying something. Nate drew close enough to see what the Reverend was shooting at.

That same far-away row of bottles only a sharpshooter could hit.

Why bother giving pointers to a man who ignores every one of them? He started to walk away, until he heard *Bang! Crash!*

Was that the sound of a bottle breaking?

If it was, it had to be dumb luck. But then—he heard it again.

Bang! Crash!

Nate stopped and turned. The Reverend twirled the pistol on his trigger finger and dropped it with precision into his holster. A split second later, he drew again.

Another broken bottle.

What the....?

Three for three, and those were no ordinary shots.

That can't be the Reverend.

But if not him, then who? Who else would be wearing a black suit and riding the Reverend's horse?

Maybe a better question was—who'd be cold-blooded enough to kill a member of the clergy and steal his horse? From behind, the man was tall and slim, the same size as the Reverend, but a lot calmer—and a lot cockier. In fact, he was just about the same size and shape as Tom Drown, the man who'd shot Beaufort.

Nate dove behind an acacia tree. The thorny shoots growing out of the trunk stabbed his chin, but he lay on his belly, still as a wide-eyed rabbit.

The gunfire stopped. Had he been spotted? Hoping he wouldn't find the barrel of a Colt pointed at him, he peered out.

To his relief, he saw the man was just reloading his pistol. But from this angle, Nate also saw the face.

The Reverend faced the targets, barely specks in the distance, and drew. *Bang! Crash!* A twirl and then holster. It was lightning fast. Then, he got even faster. *Bang! Crash!* Twirl. *Bang! Crash!* Twirl. *Bang! Crash!* Twirl.

Nate had never seen anything like it.

He might now live in a city where guns were as rare as elephants, but he'd grown up in Ramsden where guns were a part of a man's apparel as common as his hat and his boots. A man's hat protected him from whatever came at him from the sky, a man's boots from whatever came at him from the ground, and a gun from whatever came from in between. Every man his father employed was required to be able to shoot adequately. But his father paid good money to hire extra protection, because driving five thousand head of cattle through the middle of nowhere meant a good chance of encountering cougars, Comanche, and cattle rustlers.

Nate had seen the best gunmen. Or thought he had up until today.

This is no ordinary man. Much less a clumsy Reverend. So why was he playing the fool? One answer was obvious—because he wanted to make sure no one knew how well he could shoot.

Stiffened by the best shooting he'd ever seen—and worse, the person he'd seen it from—Nate backed away from his hiding spot—and hightailed away. He ran until he was winded, and a cluster of rocks offered a place to sit down and think. This so-called "Reverend" had given him plenty to think about.

Those sharp-shooting skills didn't come overnight. He must have been sneaking away for years to practice. And because I was sneaking around I discovered his secret.

The Reverend must have decided to practice at the break of dawn instead. He obviously didn't want anyone to know he was a crack shot.

Questions about the Reverend began to make some sense, such as why he took a job in small-town Ramsden. This man had found a good way to hide in the open by wearing a black suit with a white collar and acting like he had two left hands dipped in butter.

Today's encounter kicked up a dust devil of new questions. *Who* was the man hiding in the clergy suit? *What* was he hiding—beyond the fact he was a deadeye? And if he was willing to risk even a ghost of a chance of being caught shooting, he didn't want to get rusty, so—*What's he still hiding now?*

Nate's blood ran cold.

Hattie, what did you get mixed up with?

7

Sitting on a rock in the middle of nowhere, Nate dragged a hand through his hair. The "Reverend" was a dangerous man and that put Hattie in peril. She had to be warned. But how?

If Nate told her that her clumsy beau was a deadeye, she'd accuse Nate of being crazy and jealous. In fact, if Nate went back to her house after she'd threatened to tell the sheriff, he'd likely land in jail. And telling the Reverend to stay away from her wasn't an option. A man corrupt enough to hide in a clergy suit was the type who'd eliminate a problem with a bullet. The Reverend wouldn't appreciate someone knowing his secret, and Nate could never outshoot him.

How could Nate save a damsel in distress who wasn't willing to be rescued—especially when he was the dragon she wanted to be rescued from?

But Hattie was no helpless damsel. She'd proven time again that she was a resourceful bobcat of a woman bold enough to go against a bear. He'd seen her take a gun right out of man's hand back when she'd worked in the saloon.

Nate dropped his hand between his knees. Maybe the best thing to do was to leave a capable Hattie to her own resources and to move on. He had a job to get back to, and she'd made it clear she didn't want him barging into her miserable life like a prince on a steed to sweep her off to his faraway castle.

Hattie. She'd come a long way from the little girl who'd stolen his heart, the one who'd once needed his rescuing—or a boy's attempt at rescuing her, anyway. He smiled sadly at the memory of the first time he'd seen her.

"Who are you?" the teacher asked a thin, six-year-old girl who'd walked into the schoolhouse long after everyone else was seated.

"Hattie Brown, ma'am," she'd said in a quiet voice.

"What are you doing here?"

"I'd like to come to school if you please, ma'am."

"School started three weeks and fifteen minutes ago. Why are you so late?"

"My maw needed me at home, ma'am."

The teacher hesitated. "Go find a seat."

She chose the one next to Nate, and sat down. She was so unique. Her skin was olive, her braids were blacker than black, and her eyes were large and dark and hard to look away from. She caught Nate staring at her and smiled at him so prettily, he could have sworn she was a princess from a far-away country, had it not been for her burlap dress.

Later, he found out it was made out of a flour sack, and it itched her all day long. As if things weren't miserable enough for her, the children started poking fun at her.

"Stay away from Hattie Brown," they taunted. "She's got fleas."

She never said a word back, and the ridicule continued until her pretty smile began to fade.

Each day found him wishing she'd come to school wearing something different, only to be disappointed to find her wearing the same itchy, albeit clean, dress.

Finally, when the days of ridicule took away her smile altogether, he set his mind to fix things for her. Nate's plan was that of a child's. He would take it as far as he could go, and trust God to bring it to a fairytale ending.

God seemed to test Nate's determination as Nate sneaked off early one Saturday morning. It was chilly, and he hadn't brought his coat. His boots were new and chafed his feet raw. But he wouldn't turn back. This was for Hattie so she could smile again.

When he reached her home, what he saw took him by surprise. He'd never seen anyone work so hard for what little they had. Clotheslines crossed the property, and he passed through veils of overalls, shirts, and bed sheets. He found Hattie stooped over a bucket scrubbing clothes against a washboard. She stopped when she saw him.

"That ain't enough scrubbing," Mrs. Brown said. "Scrub some more."

It was the first time Nate had ever seen an African woman up close, and he stared at her. She looked at her daughter and then what her daughter was looking at. Mrs. Brown's eyes peered at him like two big pearls. "What do you want here, boy?"

"May I speak to Hattie, ma am?"

Mrs. Brown huffed and left them to hang up some clothes. She had good reason to dislike the Powells. Nate's mother claimed she'd do the clothes herself before she'd let Mrs. Brown touch them. It wasn't Mrs. Brown's color; it was the fact that there was no Mr. Brown that Nate's mother sputtered on about.

"Hello, Hattie," Nate said.

Hattie made sure her mother was out of earshot before setting aside the shirt she'd been scrubbing. Her burlap dress was as soaked as the clothes she was washing. If it was cold for Nate, it was too cold for a girl that thin to be that wet. But even being wet and cold and wearing an itchy dress, her face lit up as he approached her.

"Howdy, Nate." Her teeth chattered, but the smile that returned to her pretty face was even more radiant than the first time he'd seen it. It sent a ray clear through to his heart, and he was sure it lit up his face as well.

He cleared his throat. *"Would you wash this for me?"* He handed her a shirt that had already been laundered, because that wasn't the point. *"I can pay you."* He extended a fist full of money, every cent he had. *"Here. Maybe you can buy yourself a new dress."*

Nate stared into the stillness. It was strange how Hattie had evolved from a girl with a burlap dress and an angelic smile to a saint wearing a high-neck calico dress, because of the woman wedged in between.

She'd once worn the off-the-shoulder dress of a saloon girl.

He'd never considered her the immoral woman folks had accused her of being. She may have drawn the line further than she should have when she'd taken on the job, but when she'd established that line, it was more like a moat. In a town dominated by love-sick men and a stop along the way for love-starved cowboys, she could have made a fortune selling herself. But she didn't. And no man dared ask her twice.

Nate had never asked her once. Her self-respect relied on her virtue, and he couldn't take it away from her. By not taking her virtue from her, he'd only grown to admire her more. *I'll never stop loving you, Hattie.* Doing so would mean giving up all the good that was ever in him. There were times she made him the man he wanted to be.

There was always good in Hattie, and there'd always be. For the Reverend to have tricked someone as astute as her, he was as good at acting as he was at shooting, because Hattie would never take part in such a deception.

Hattie, I know you can fend for yourself against anything. If she knew what she was fending herself against.

He glanced in the direction that would take him back to a safe but lonely life. Then he glanced toward a town haunted with memories. His hands trembled a warning to stay away from Ramsden. But he tucked them under his arms and began to walk toward the lion's den.

8

Hattie put her pies in the oven, wiped some sweat off her brow, and hung her potholder on a nail head. She heaved a sigh at the kitchen bench encrusted with dough, potato peels, and chicken bones. Since Nate had come back and offered her a way out, pie baking was beginning to feel like less of a job and more of a drudge. She looked down at her faded dress and remembered that, for some reason, Nate had always cared about what she wore.

She sat in a rocking chair, knowing she should be spending this time patching a hole in the henhouse. But while her pies were baking, she took some time to rock and remember a time back when her dresses weren't so modestly high on the neck.

~*~

"So, where're you headed off to, Nate?"

"I'll be back in a week or two."

Achy didn't begin to describe how each passing day felt without seeing him. Hoping to see him walk into the saloon, she'd look at the scarred door that cooped her up seven days a week. One week without seeing him felt like a year. Two weeks passed, and she found it difficult to smile for the belching, sweating customers who smelled more sour than the horse droppings they brought in with them on their boots.

Then two weeks and one day too long passed. Had some other woman taken him away?

He was a gentleman, always clean shaven and neatly dressed. He never cussed, not even the time his horse stepped on his foot. And with his wavy blond hair, chiseled jaw, and blue eyes he was finer looking than any man she'd ever seen. He looked more like a picture of Eros she'd once seen in a mythology book. And he was smart as a whip.

Why would he want to marry you, Hattie Brown? You're nothing but a two-bit saloon gal who doesn't even own a proper dress. The yellow dress, the one she wore the most because it was her best, had four faded red and green plaid patches on it. Plaid and yellow. It mixed as well as her and Nate.

Two weeks and two days passed. She spent a quiet day staring at the door.

That evening brought in the regulars and more than the usual share of men passing through and stopping at the only saloon in town. It also brought in a stranger who decided he liked the bar stool one of the locals was sitting in. The stranger grabbed old Malachi by the scruff of the shirt and threw him off.

While Malachi, a peaceful and cockeyed old goat, limped over to another stool, Hattie eyed the stranger. He was a bull of a man looking for trouble, so she coined him Mr. Trouble. She knew the type. Someone who had to prove with his fists that he was bigger than everyone else because he was too stupid to judge he was a head taller and a belt notch wider. She also knew it wasn't wise to get that sort too drunk because they only got meaner.

But the man came in with a bulging pouch of money he'd set on the bar—and Hattie's boss caught sight of it. She didn't want to talk sweet to a man who'd done that to Malachi, but flirting with men to buy drinks so Boss could get their money was her job. Or part of it, anyway. Keeping peace in the saloon and seeing to it that the mirror didn't get busted was the other half of her responsibility.

Although a mirror made the place look nicer, its real purpose was for the staff to keep an eye on customers in case they drew a gun or started tearing up the place—and why Boss invested so much money in one. In fact, he had invested such a fortune in it, neither Hattie nor the bartender dared to put a smudge on the glass or even touch its ornate walnut frame.

The doors swung open again. Her heart fluttered.

Nate!

After two and a half weeks, he'd come back all duded up in a suit, vest, and tie. He carried a fancy box with him.

She wanted to run to him, but Boss caught her attention and jerked his head, signaling her to flirt with Mr. Trouble.

She slung her arm around Mr. Trouble's shoulder but kept her eye and smile on Nate as he walked through the crowd, over to the only empty table, and set the box on it. With a smirk, he crossed his arms. He'd wait as long as it took until she could come around to him—and see what was in the box.

She wanted to get rid of Mr. Trouble quickly, so she called to the bartender, "Mel, set us up with two glasses of your best whisky." Then she said to Mr. Trouble, "Think you're man enough to drink dollar-a-glass whisky?"

Mel planted two glasses on the bar, one filled with their best whisky, and for Hattie, a glass of water mixed with sarsaparilla to color it amber. She hoped Mr. Trouble's money ran out before his thirst did.

He thrust back his head and downed the shot.

Mel was busy catering to the cranky, thirsty crowd while Boss stood on the sidelines socializing.

She poured Mr. Trouble another expensive whisky and took care of some of Mel's orders as well. But all the while she kept looking over at Nate and at the box he'd brought in, all tied up pretty with ribbon. If the box was that fancy, what could possibly be inside?

"Hattie, get me another whisky." Mr. Trouble again.

Boss cast her a narrow-eyed threat. "Keep him drinking," he mouthed. Once a man left town, so did Boss's chance of getting all his money.

She went around the bar and as she poured another, she watched Mr. Trouble's head wobble in the mirror. Then she smirked as she looked down into a glass of the same whisky everybody else was paying twenty-five cents for.

"Stop looking at me like that," Mr. Trouble barked at Malachi.

She quickly slid by his side and breathed into his ear, "You're the kind of man a gal hankers for. Look at you, so tall and strong." It calmed him. It worked on all the Mr. Troubles.

She sighed at Nate, still waiting, still without a drink, but looking content just to watch her. Watching him watching her made her smile back.

Boss didn't like her smiling at Nate. He jerked his head toward another customer to keep her busy. But the moment she left Mr. Trouble's side, he riled up again.

"I said, stop looking at me like that." He flung a stool over the bar toward the mirror.

Hattie's heart throbbed in her throat as Mel handed her the stool Mr. Trouble had thrown. A bead of sweat trickled down Mel's brow, but it wasn't there for his sake. It was there for hers. If something happened to that mirror...

She set the stool down where it belonged, but it took a moment longer to calm her nerves. "What's the matter with you?" she demanded of Mr. Trouble.

"I don't like the way he's looking at me."

She followed Mr. Trouble's glare to cockeyed old Malachi. "For Pete's sake," she said, "the man can't help it. He's got one eye looking this-a-way and one eye looking that-a-way, so it doesn't matter who you are or where you're standing because he always looks like he's got one eye on everybody everywhere." She planted her hands on her hips.

Mr. Trouble was nothing but a big man itching for a fight, and Malachi had the misfortune of being singled out.

She'd liked to have kicked him out, but Boss wouldn't have allowed it. So she did what she could to keep the peace. With the tip of her finger, she turned the man's head from Malachi's crazy eyes toward hers. "How about you look at me instead?" She winked at him and his eyes lighted up in his broad, bearded face.

She went behind the bar to get beers for a table of customers who were cussing at the bartender for moving too slowly. "Here you go, boys. And for waiting so long..." She gave each a thrill by taking a kiss-like sip from their mugs.

She kept distracting Mr. Trouble from Malachi by winking at him. She earned everyone else's attention and some wolf calls by swaying her hips. It gave her and Mel the opportunity to get the drinks everyone had been clamoring for until everybody was happy. And that gave her a chance to do what she'd been hankering for.

"Here you go." She set a glass in front of Nate and sat in the chair across from him. She pulled her black hair forward on her shoulder knowing he liked it that way. She nodded toward the box. "Who's that for?"

His cheeks dimpled. "You know who it's for."

Her face heated. He was the only man who'd ever made her blush. "What are you buying me presents for? Are you trying to buy my affections?" She gave him a half smirk, because he knew better. Hattie Brown may have flaunted her wares, but they weren't for sale.

"Are you going to see what's inside?" he said. "Or just admire the box?"

"I'd like to admire the box for a while, if you don't mind. I've never seen anything so fine."

"That's because you've never seen yourself from behind my eyes."

She looked at his face framed by playful curls and then into eyes as serene as a Texas summer sky. Nate was as appealing as a man could be, yet he'd never overstepped his bounds with her, never acted uncomely. What exactly was he thinking behind those eyes? Was it too much to hope he was thinking the same thing she was but was too afraid to say, because if he didn't say it back…?

She looked down. If he didn't say it back, her heart would cave in on her. "Let's see what's in this box." She tugged the end of a big red bow, lifted the cover off, and what she found inside took her breath away.

It was the prettiest dress she'd ever seen—red satin with enough fabric on the bustle to clothe every woman from Ramsden to Kansas City. It must have cost him a fortune. "Nate. I…" He was also the only man who'd ever rendered her speechless.

"It's a gift for me as well as it is for you," he said.

"And why is that?" She recovered her voice enough to tease him. "So you can enjoy 'the view' better?"

"Because that dress you're wearing has patches on it. I don't like to see you wearing rags, Hattie. Now go upstairs and put this on."

She kissed him and rushed off to put on the new dress.

She tore off the old, patched dress and put on the new. She looked at her image in the looking glass. "Now ain't you something, Hattie Brown."

The new dress made her look more like a fancy stage

singer than the two-bit saloon girl she was. Her smile was as broad as could be. She turned to see what the back looked like and lost her smile.

It wasn't what the back of the dress looked like that saddened her; it was what her skin looked like. She tugged the dress so that it covered the gouges and scabby scars she didn't want Nate to see.

Looking at the front view again gave her back her smile. She glowed in this dress. She couldn't wait to show it off to Nate.

It wasn't until she headed down the stairs that she realized the five minutes she'd been gone was ten seconds too long.

Thump. "Quit looking at me that way!"

Whack. "Leave the man alone!"

Thud. "Mind your business."

Boom. "He is my business."

And then came the worst sound of them all.

Crash!

Hattie froze in her steps.

Nate never got to see what the dress looked like on her that night because that was the sound of Boss's mirror getting busted.

Boss fired a shot and cleared out the saloon early that night.

As Mel swept the glass, Boss glared at her. "Get back upstairs, Hattie. I need to have a talk with you about spending too much time with Nate."

Those were the words she'd dreaded, because Boss didn't lash her with his tongue.

Tears burned Hattie's eyes as she touched the small of her back. Through the thin cotton she could still feel the scarred gouges Boss's belt buckle had left behind almost a decade earlier. Beatings Nate never knew about. Beatings he would have saved her from had he asked her to marry him way back when.

The hand-me-down dresses she now wore came with the house she'd inherited from an old Christian widow who'd taken pity on her. This was how Hattie had gotten out of the saloon and away from Boss, not by marrying Nate as she'd hoped. She'd also inherited, along with everything else the widow had, the recipe for chicken pie.

A home, a way to make a living, the right kind of clothes to wear. They all witnessed to Hattie who had rescued her in the end.

You had your chance, Nate. It would have saved her a lot of grief had he taken it.

9

Nate walked past thigh-high bushes of snakeweed. His gut warned him to turn back, but his heart urged him toward downtown Ramsden and a solution to warn Hattie about the Reverend. *If I can't tell her that the Reverend isn't as pious as he appears to be, I know who she'll listen to.*

Sheriff Breck had always been respected by everyone, and he'd always gotten to the bottom of a matter even when the matter sounded absurd. An old recluse had complained that his house was haunted because coins were disappearing. While everyone laughed, Breck scrutinized the house until he found the ghost to be a thieving packrat. Accusing a fumbling Reverend of being a deadeye would sound just as ludicrous, but Breck was sure to get to the bottom of that matter as well—where he was sure to find another rat.

The morning sun glared past the narrow rim of Nate's stylish but impractical derby hat and in his eyes. Blisters on his feet throbbed. Working at a desk inside a building had turned him into a tenderfoot. There was a time when he'd lived out here for months at a time. That, however, was not of his choosing.

A memory of the year he'd turned fourteen wormed its way through the boredom. He'd been reading when his father walked in on him and snatched the book away.

"'How do I love thee?'" His father had quit school in the third grade and read choppily. "'Let me count the ways.' What kind of nonsense you reading here, son?"

"It's not nonsense. It's a poem by Elizabeth Barrett Browning."

"Elizabeth? You're reading a book written by a woman?" His father closed the book. "Books like that ain't going to do you no good."

Nate had made a promise to his teacher. "Miss Clake's taken sick and she asked me to teach class for her, so-"

"So she can find one of the girls to do it for her. Get your head out of the clouds. Man's got to learn how to make a living and that's why you're coming on this next cattle drive." Marcus Powell was the most successful rancher in the county, and once a year he and his hired hands would drive five thousand cattle to the train station in Dodge City.

"But I don't want to drive cattle. I want to be a teacher."

"I didn't ask what you wanted to be, son, I'm telling you what you're going to do." His father started walking away, which meant the conversation was over. Or almost over. He had one more thing to add. "While we're out there, I want you to keep a good eye on my point rider. Zachariah's the same age as you, and he's as good as they come."

A cactus snagged Nate's sleeve, and he pulled himself free. There was a river nearby, and he abruptly steered off the path for a refreshing drink. But when he returned to the path, thoughts of Marcus were there waiting for him.

Marcus. Nate wouldn't call that man "father" again, least of all pay him a visit. Not after where Marcus had sent him, though more than likely, Marcus had simply told everyone that he'd sent Nate back East to live with his aunt.

Nate snorted. He didn't live with Aunt Sarah, she just took care of business, and when it was over she gave Nate a stack of letters she'd collected for him while he was "away" as she'd called it.

There were five years' worth of letters. The ones from Marcus were postdated the first three years, and then his mother wrote some later. Nate learned that Hattie had moved into that old shack, and that Marcus had promoted Zachariah. Nate tired of reading about cowboys like they were heroes, and lovers of books like they were fools. Sickened by his father's boasts about how skillful Zachariah was, Nate had tossed the rest of the unopened letters into the fireplace, including the ones from his mother whom he'd assumed wrote on Marcus's behalf because Nate never wrote back.

Nate had always been and always would be a failure in his father's eyes, because the way Marcus measured success was by how well a man could ride and rope and how much he knew about cattle. Marcus made it clear that Zachariah measured up, and Nate never would.

Nate's eyes burned. *Just one more day in this God-forsaken place.* Tomorrow would find him on his way back to the prestigious job, the impressive house, and the elite acquaintances that included him in their parties. But a place he could never call home.

He looked at the Texas sky, wide above his head. Massachusetts had an altogether different sky, made smaller by giant oaks and maples. He didn't look up there often. But although the sky here was familiar, he couldn't call Ramsden home either. Home was a place that wanted a person. A place that evoked good memories. Home was where someone belonged, and he didn't belong here. Because Ramsden was where

Zachariah belonged.

Everything. That's what Zachariah took from him. His father's love, and then Hattie. Nate hadn't become engaged to Lillian out of love, but out of revenge. He had attempted to steal her from Zachariah, so that Zachariah would never find happiness.

~*~

Oh no.

Hattie had gone outside with a hammer, some nails, and a board to patch the hole in the henhouse at the wrong moment.

"I see you could use some help." The Reverend seemed always to catch her at her worst—when she was fixing things. But even that wasn't the worst of it.

"Be careful of—" Hattie started, but she was too late.

He tripped over one chicken and staggered over another until they were all in a rumpus, squawking at him. The man was lanky and gangly and it seemed his arms and legs were so long his mind couldn't keep track of his hands and feet. Then, to top things off, he took the hammer from her.

"If you hold the nail," the Reverend said, "I'll—"

Before another disaster could happen, she snatched the hammer back. "How about if *I* swing the hammer and *you* hold the nail?" She needed her fingers unbroken more than she needed the henhouse fixed. Besides it wasn't so much to keep the chickens from getting out as it was to keep the foxes from getting in. And even that was questionable, as Hattie's scarred-up arms attested. Any fox that dared to get near this brood of killer hens would scurry out just as fast as it had scurried in. She disguised her apprehension of doing things the other way around. "You think a woman can't swing a hammer?"

The Reverend pushed his eyeglasses up his nose. "I suppose..."

She laid the board flat on the ground and tapped two nails into either end of it first. Then she put it against the henhouse. "Here. Just hold the board still." She closed her eyes with frustration.

He couldn't even do that right.

"Your face," she said. "Either you'll have to move it to the side, or I'll smash those eyeglasses of yours." Which wouldn't be a loss, since they didn't seem to do much except make him look like a befuddled owl.

He focused on the board, as if he had to count every knot in order to hold it there.

Hattie held her tongue. Intelligence was something to admire in a man—even if the Reverend was more book-learning than common sense.

He moved his head to the side, and she started hammering. Less than four strikes later, the board he was supposed to be holding steady had slipped out of place. She stopped and politely readjusted it. "Reverend," she said when she was ready to start hammering again, "please move your face." She managed to nail in one end of the board, even though it had slipped so that it was slightly askew of the hole. But it was close enough to the place she wanted it—or rather, she was too frustrated to try to correct it—and so it was time to switch places with him so she could nail in the other end. But they kept getting in each other's way.

"How about if I...?" He started to move in one direction as she started to move in another. It only resulted in them being entwined with one another, with their faces inches apart.

He backed away from her and let go of the board he was supposed to be holding.

It was a good thing she'd managed to attach the one side because it swung vertically.

"Put your hand here." She took control by swinging the board back into place and planting his hand on the end that needed steadying. "Now don't move." She walked around him. She pulled back the hammer to strike. "You've got to move your face out of the way, Reverend."

He shifted his face as well as the board.

She hammered in the nail. "I reckon that just about does it." If she wanted to save her sanity, she'd better put off patching the henhouse until after he'd left. Then she could get it done right in a fraction of the time it was taking them to do it wrong together. And she still had to get her pies over to Kate's. "Thank you for stopping by, Reverend. I'll see you at church Sunday."

That was a hint that it was time for him to leave. However, after she sat in the wagon and took the reins, he was still standing there. "Is there something else, Reverend?"

"We're not done fixing the hole yet. I—"

"I could sure use a glass of sarsaparilla. How about if you come to Kate's with me, and I'll treat you to a glass to thank you for helping me fix the henhouse?" She didn't have to worry about the man thinking she was being forward or thinking anything romantic at all. She'd known him for seven years, and they'd never even held hands. He was as romantic as the mumps. She wanted a man who gave her goose bumps. A man like…no, she wouldn't allow herself to even think his name.

The Reverend glanced back at the unfinished patch. "But it's not—"

"It's fixed good enough for now, Reverend." It came out louder than she'd intended. "Now get in."

~*~

Nate climbed a hill of loose sand made even more hazardous by patches of prickly pears. He'd sneaked into town by a path he'd used only once before—and that was when he'd brought a rifle along to kill Zachariah.

Nate made his way to the top of the hill where he could see the town buildings below, including the new telegraph office. They'd put in a larger window when they'd rebuilt it after the fire.

The fire he'd set.

Memories of that long-ago event stabbed at him. After Lillian had confessed she loved Zachariah, Nate's lust for revenge escalated into blind rage. Instead of shooting Zachariah, circumstances offered Nate an opportunity for greater retribution when Lillian walked into the telegraph office. Clayton, the telegrapher, had just finished varnishing the walls, and when Clayton left her alone inside, well, the last thing Nate remembered was the flare as he slipped in, lit a match, and set the wall aflame.

To this day, he didn't know if Lillian had made it out alive, because he didn't wake up in Ramsden. He woke up in Independence, Iowa. He clutched his head and fell to his knees in a swirl of turmoil. Until one word brought him back.

Hattie.

He stole his way to his last cover, a hedge of prickly pear. He'd have to slide down the hill and then dash across open space before finding cover again behind the town buildings. The sheriff's office was just across the street, and that would be the end of Nate's trouble. He'd tell Breck about the Reverend, purchase a horse from the livery, and hightail out of this den of bad memories.

He peered out at Main Street, quiet but for a few pedestrians. Yes, this would go smoothly. Something stirred some dust—a wagon heading toward town—so he ducked and waited for it to pass. The horse moved as slowly as growing grass. Finally, creaking wheels and whiffs of a horse reached him, and he peered out to see who might be driving it.

Hattie—*and* the Reverend.

Nate wanted to yank that lying sack away from her but forced himself to wait. The solution was moments away. A tapping on his boot caught his attention. He looked down. He was standing in a nest of scorpions.

10

Nate leaped away, and a split second later, something flew out of the wagon.

"I dropped my hat," the Reverend said to Hattie. "Would you…?"

Nate scampered back behind the hedge. Had the Reverend spotted him? A man who could shoot as well as the Reverend would have the eyesight of an eagle. Was dropping his hat just an excuse to look around?

Her voice dripped with irritation as Hattie called out, "Hold on there, Nellie."

The wagon below came to a halt.

The Reverend jumped off. He walked up to his hat and kicked it toward the incline—in Nate's direction.

Nate crouched low. Was *I know you're hiding something* written in the sweat that dampened his shirt or whispered in his heavy breathing? Was his heart pounding it out in Morse code?

A large scorpion crawled onto the back of his hand. He flicked it off before it could sting him. But a dozen more were climbing up. He swallowed as the insects he'd always hated crept up his trousers, their segmented and curled stingers ready to strike. The sting smarted like a branding iron. And the ugly pests made his flesh crawl.

"Sorry, Hattie, but my hat keeps getting away from me." The Reverend was still close by.

All the scorpions were now on Nate. One crawled

onto his neck with a prickle, and he held back every muscle itching to spring out and brush it off. A crunch of sand said that the Reverend was just on the other side of the hedge. Another crunch, and Nate and the Reverend were eye to deadly eye.

Nate's throat was too dry to swallow. Every drop in his body had turned to sweat.

"Reverend," Hattie called. "Did you get your hat back?"

If you hurt her...

The Reverend stared at Nate and then plucked his hat off the ground. "I caught up to it. Must have been the wind." Was that the sound of one outlaw covering for another?

If it was, Hattie didn't notice. "Must have been." Her voice bristled at the frayed end of her tolerance. How could she not see through his foolishness? "Now Reverend, if you'd kindly get back in the wagon, I need to get these pies over to Kate's."

The Reverend released Nate's glare and then played the clumsy oaf climbing back into the wagon. The lazy thuds of the horse faded away.

"Ouch!" A scorpion stung him on the neck. Another stung him on the wrist. Nate managed to brush the rest of them off. The stings burned. But not as much as the encounter with the Reverend. Nate's skin prickled with unease that had nothing to do with insects.

~*~

Hattie halted the horse in front of the wooden building with the big window and the sign that read "Kate's Eatery." She had a potential disaster on her hands. To immediately head off the calamity, she jumped off the bench, rushed to the back of the wagon, and grabbed two pies. She gave neither Zachariah nor Clayton enough time to offer their help, because someone else was bound to offer.

"May I help—"

"No, thank you, Reverend."

He was such a stumblebum that if he helped, there were bound to be some pies that didn't make it. She brought the pies to the door just as Kate opened it. Hattie shoved the pies at Kate and whispered, "Set these down quick and meet me at the door again."

Kate's eyes grew wide when she saw the Reverend, and she snatched the pies to set them on the closest table. She skedaddled back to receive the next two from Hattie.

The Reverend started getting down from the wagon. "Are you sure I can't—" He caught his sleeve on the brake handle.

"Kate and I are doing just fine, Reverend," Hattie said, though Kate was beginning to look winded. Hattie handed Kate the next two.

He tried to tug free. "But we could get it done faster if I—"

"Almost done."

His predicament was a blessing.

Hattie grabbed more pies as he twisted and tugged.

"I seem to be caught—"

"Be there in a minute." Hattie shoved the pies at Kate and turned.

The Reverend had managed to free himself and was stepping off the wagon to get that final pie.

Hattie beat him to it and delivered the last pie safe

and sound, though Kate looked ruffled.

~*~

Nate dashed to the back of the town buildings and then slipped up the alley between the general store and the telegraph office. The sheriff's office was across the street. The businesses were just opening and there were only a few people around. He waited for the barber standing in his doorway to greet a customer and for a woman who led her child into the general store. A couple of women walked along the boardwalk and disappear into another building.

Breck—he's still the sheriff, isn't he?

When Nate lived here, the man had complained that he was getting old and had talked about giving up his badge. But Breck had been saying that for years. Surely, he cared too much about this town to quit.

Now.

Someone came out of the sheriff's office.

Nate stopped short.

Zachariah.

Nate's heart pounded at the sight of tall, dark-haired, know-it-all Zachariah. He'd put on a few years and added some bulk, but he still had that patch of rippled, maroon-stained skin right smack on his face, that ever-present reminder to Nate of what his sister had looked like after she'd burned to death.

Nate threw himself back in the alley and leaned against a building until he caught his breath. A few moments later, Nate peered around the corner.

Zachariah had settled on the bench in front of the sheriff's office.

Go home. Go to work. Go anywhere but here.

Zachariah perched his feet up on the horse rail and got more comfortable—as comfortable as he had the day Nate had set out to kill him—but had instead set fire to the building Lillian was in.

A fire for a fire.

Death of Zachariah's woman for the death of Nate's sister.

Nate threw his hands over his face. He stumbled into the rough brick wall.

Control. He couldn't lose control for Hattie's sake. He'd have to wait for Zachariah to leave before he could talk to Sheriff Breck.

Zachariah still hadn't budged.

Nate punched the brick. *Don't you have somewhere else to be?* The answer came back with a flash of sunlight on silver.

The sheriff's badge glowed on Zachariah's vest.

11

Hattie and the Reverend sat at a table covered with a red checkered tablecloth by a window draped with matching curtains. They sipped on their glasses of cool sarsaparilla. The Reverend's gaze locked onto the window and hers fastened onto old Malachi and his English wife, Rosie. Rosie had him wearing suits and ties and top hats nothing like the old cowhide duds he'd worn before he'd married her.

"How many times do I have to tell you to take off your hat when you're sitting at the table?" Rosie harped in her English accent. "Don't anything sink into that gray noggin of yours?"

"Yes, my sweet blossom." He plucked off his hat and put it in his lap. "I forgot."

"And get your elbows off the table. A gentleman don't eat like that."

"Yes, honeysuckle. I'm sorry." Even after seven years of marriage, Malachi, an old hermit who'd struck gold, still adored his fancy English mail-order bride.

Privately, Hattie always thought Rosie wanted to make an Arabian stallion out of a mule. But at least Malachi and Rosie were talking to one another. Even after seven years of knowing him, not only did Hattie and the Reverend not talk, but she only knew him as the Reverend.

Men. Why were the ones who mattered such strangers? Or like Nate, who'd hurt her? Her chest felt heavy as if she'd swallowed a lump of lead. There were two men whose absence in her life had left her wounded.

Nate—and her father.

The Reverend was still looking out the window but at least not spilling or causing confusion. How did he feel about her? Did he even find her attractive? Everyone said that the way he tripped and fumbled around her was a sure sign he was taken by her, but he did that around everybody. And there were times when his clumsiness seemed a bit—unusually coordinated.

He was tall and slim and if he didn't slouch, maybe he wouldn't look so lanky. He had a straight nose, a square jaw, and a thick crop of dark brown hair, which might look comely if he parted it on the side instead of in the middle.

She'd known him for seven years but hardly knew him at all.

How many siblings did he have? What was his favorite food, his favorite color?

Nate had had just the one sister, and his favorite food was steak and mashed potatoes with creamed corn and apple pie for dessert. His favorite color was yellow. He'd told her that one day when he'd brought her a dozen yellow roses. *"They're so pretty, Nate,"* she'd said. *"Pretty, yes,"* he'd answered. *"But nothing's as beautiful as you are."*

She sighed at the ache brought by the memory. Why was she always lonely for the men who'd made her heart feel as if it'd been carved out and stomped on? There'd been another man in her life besides Nate, and he'd hurt her just as badly.

Her pa.

It had been difficult growing up without a father. There was nobody to provide for her and her ma. Her ma scrubbed away at more than just the dirt on the clothes she'd washed for a living. She and Hattie took turns.

~*~

"Ma," Hattie said as she dipped some stranger's dirty long johns into a steaming washtub. Though her hands were red, she'd gotten used to the heat. "Where's my pa?"

Her mother, rag tied around her head, was hanging a shirt on the clothesline but stopped. "He's dead." She tossed the shirt back at Hattie. "Now you'd best scrub that collar better than that."

Hattie finished the long johns and took up the poorly-washed shirt. "How'd he die?"

Her ma huffed. "Civil War took him." She folded the long johns over the line and pinned them.

"What'd he look like?"

"What you think he looked like? He had two eyes, a nose, and a mouth just like every other man. Now stop talking and start scrubbing. We got to get these clothes back to the saloon by tomorrow morning."

There was always a pile of laundry waiting for the washtub and a deadline to do it in that cut short their conversations about her pa. But no matter how many clothes they washed, the pile never got smaller. Her ma would send Hattie off to bed, but Hattie would watch her from the window, still working by the light of a kerosene lamp in the night chill with bed sheets billowing like ghosts from her past. Hattie's eyes would mist, wishing she had a pa to make her life feel safer and her ma's life easier. She even prayed he'd somehow survived the war and that he'd come back for them.

She got half her miracle.

~*~

Zachariah's the sheriff now?

Nate pounded the building's side until the gritty brick bruised his fists and scuffed his knuckles. He sagged against the wall. The man he wanted to avoid was the man he needed to talk to. How could he protect Hattie from the Reverend when he couldn't talk to the sheriff?

A man unscrupulous enough to hide behind a pulpit was the type of man deceitful enough to hide a dangerous secret. And with the skills to back up whatever that secret was...

Think. He needed more time to come up with something to help Hattie. But too much time meant missing the stagecoach and the day he was due back at work. A position as vice president of the most prestigious bank in Boston wasn't a job a man wanted to lose. He looked at the red brick before him, hit it again, and then leaned his forehead on his fist. Hattie had always been there when he'd needed her. For the first time in her life, she needed him even if she didn't know it. Nate would extend his stay by notifying his employer he'd been delayed. All he had to do was slip around the corner and into the door of the very building he'd been striking.

Zachariah lifted his feet off the horse rail and went inside the sheriff's office.

Nate drew a breath and walked out of the alley. Just before he rounded the corner into the telegraph office, a child shot out of the general store.

"Molly," a woman shouted from inside the store.

Before the child could get too far, Nate scooped her up. "Hold on there." She was a little thing in a crisply ironed dress with black hair and pretty blue eyes. Before he could put the child down, her mother came rushing out of the store after her.

"Mol—" The mother came to a dead standstill the moment she saw Nate.

He froze as though he'd seen an apparition.

Lillian, the woman he'd trapped in the burning building, gaped at him. She was petite, black-haired, and pale with fear.

He couldn't stammer a word, knowing he'd been the devil to her.

"Y-You're back," she stammered.

Even if she knew nothing about his attempt to kill her, he'd given her reason to fear when he'd tried to force her to marry him. This place was cursed with reminders of what kind of man he'd been.

"Lillian, I…" He wanted to quell her fear, to plead his apology.

Her eyes were wide as she looked at him holding her child.

Terror was in Lillian's eyes. The terror of seeing a raging beast who'd tried to use her as the club with which to bludgeon Zachariah.

His monster was merely slumbering within and tied with a very thin rope. The only peace offering he could tender was to put the child down. "Go to your mother."

Lillian reached out and pulled the little girl away from Nate. She pushed the child behind her and stood like a mother rabbit between her kit and a mountain lion. Her bravery made him even more ashamed.

"I see you're married." It was a feeble attempt to put her at ease and acknowledge her condition: foremost alive but furthermore rounded with another child well on the way. "I assume to Zachariah?"

"You assume correctly. He's the sheriff now." That statement wasn't so much an update of her husband's occupation as it was a warning.

"You have my congratulations. Good day—Mrs. Keane." He turned to escape from her and the memories she stirred.

Zachariah stepped out of the sheriff's office.

Nate nearly ran into the telegraph office. He'd been wrong about fate finally befriending him. Seeing Lillian...and Zachariah...had the sheriff seen Nate talking to her? A confrontation with Zachariah would be too much to handle. *Fate, please give me that much.*

"Nate? Is that you?"

A friendly voice from the past.

Nate drew a deep breath.

"Well hang me if it isn't." Clayton shot out from behind a pine desk and slapped Nate's shoulder. Seven years and having to rebuild his business had turned Clayton's brown hair to gray. "Good to see you again, Nate."

Nate shook hands with the man whose business he'd burned down. Judging by the excitement in his voice, Clayton had never figured it out. "What have you been up to? What are you doing back in town?"

"I need to send a wire." It was all Nate could manage.

"Sure. I can do that for you."

Nate wrote out the request for his employer to extend his absence.

Clayton went behind the desk and tapped it out.

The door creaked opened.

One big leather boot planted itself inside, and another followed just as firmly.

"Howdy, Clayton." Zachariah added in a flat voice, "Howdy, Nate."

12

Red mist flooded Nate's brain at the patch of rippled scarlet skin on Zachariah's face, at the reminder of Sally's gruesome death by burning. He clutched his head and turned away.

"Mind if I talk to Nate?" Zachariah asked Clayton. "In private."

"Sure, Zachariah," Clayton said. "Of course." He left.

Zachariah turned to Nate and studied him before speaking. "Will I have any problems with you and Lillian?"

Nate's head buzzed as he focused on a knot in a plank of the pine floor that looked like a bullet hole. He locked his arms across his chest to get a hold of his rage. "No, you'll not have any trouble."

"Will I have problems with you and Hattie?"

Nate could taste the sullied water of resentment gurgling at the back of his throat. He wanted to spit it out at Zachariah but instead lifted his gaze to the badge gleaming off Zachariah's vest. He was talking to the town sheriff. "No, you'll not have problems between Hattie and me. But you will have problems with someone else."

"And who might that someone else be?"

Hope trumped common sense. "The Reverend. He's not as virtuous as everyone seems to think he is."

"Then what exactly might he be?"

"A crack shot. A deadeye."

Zachariah went quiet. Would he take after the former sheriff by investigating even a crazy accusation?

Zachariah put his hands on his hips, over the guns on his holster. "How long you going to be in town, Nate?"

How could Nate have expected any help from Zachariah? "Not long."

"What're you here for?"

Being in the same room as Zachariah was like drowning. Since Nate needed to stay in Ramsden longer, he offered an excuse. "I'm here to visit my parents."

"Your *parents*?"

Nate's face heated at the inflection in Zachariah's voice. Nate wanted to spit back that he had a mother, and even though his other parent preferred Zachariah over Nate, Marcus was still his father. Nate tried not to show the rage, but if he didn't look Zachariah straight in the scarred face, the man would know he was lying. The sight of the wrinkled patch of scarlet that covered Zachariah's face from cheekbone to chin sickened Nate. "Yes, Zachariah, my *parents*."

"Then you don't know."

"Know what?"

"About your pa."

Nate clamped his mouth shut on the insults that would have otherwise poured out of him. "What about my *pa*, Zachariah?" He wanted to mock Zachariah's provincialism, poke fun at his stupidity, bring him down low. *Suffocating.* Being within sight of the man's scar was holding him underwater. Did Zachariah suspect Nate had set the telegraph office on fire to kill

Lillian? Nate wanted to leave and raised his voice, demanding an answer. "What about my pa?"

Zachariah hesitated, and then he told Nate what was wrong.

~*~

The glasses of sarsaparilla in front of Hattie and the Reverend were as empty as their conversation had been. She'd stared so long at the red and white checks on the curtains that they'd all blended into red.

The Reverend sat, prim and proper, looking out the window overlooking the dusty road. His chin nudged forward as something snagged his attention. "That man looks like he's in a hurry," he said.

With something to chat about, she followed his gaze.

Nate was on horseback, already moving fast out of town. And the man he was in a hurry to get away from was standing on the boardwalk.

Zachariah.

Hattie came to her feet. *Why wasn't Nate gone yet?* She had to talk to Zachariah. "Would you excuse me, Reverend?"

With the exception of tripping on a nail head that stuck out a quarter inch and almost bumping into two other customers when he'd come in, the Reverend had done pretty well. But when he stood to excuse her from the table, his belt buckle caught the tabletop and their glasses tumbled down. Catching her glass with both his hands and using his knee to stop his glass from rolling off the table put his long, lanky limbs in an interesting position. There something suspicious in his lightning-fast reflexes. But the way he precariously balanced on one jittery foot and the way his eyes crossed trying to see through eyeglasses that fell crooked across his nose made him look so ridiculous that she dismissed that nudging notion.

He could have used some help, and it was uncharitable of her, but she was in such a hurry to talk to Zachariah that she left the Reverend to his own devices to solve his predicament.

"What's going on?" She met Zachariah on the walk in front of the telegraph office. "Did you and Nate have words?"

Zachariah hooked his thumbs in his belt as he continued looking down the street. "We had ourselves a little conversation."

"Well, is Nate leaving? He sure took off in a hurry. Do you think he's gone for good?" Was she disappointed?

Zachariah didn't comment.

Hattie spotted Lillian in the doorway to the sheriff's office. "Is Lillian all right?" Lillian and Nate had a history, and with Lillian being so close to birthing…

"She's fine," Zachariah said. "I had her and little Molly wait in my office. I'm on my way to check up on her now."

"So if everything's fine, why do you look worried?"

He answered her question with one of his own. "How did Nate find out about you and the Reverend?"

What? Why did everyone in town think they were on the verge of getting married? "I told Nate that the Reverend was my beau so he'd leave me alone."

Zachariah rubbed his jaw. "So that's why."

"Why what?"

"Why he claimed there was a problem with the Reverend."

"What kind of problem?" Hattie asked. "Like the Reverend stepping on my foot?"

Normally Zachariah would have chuckled at that, but the furrows in his brow deepened as he watched the unsettled dust Nate's horse had left behind. "He claimed the Reverend was a crack shot, a deadeye. I'm afraid Nate's jealous, and I'm worried about you, Hattie."

"Nate's watched me flirt with men for years. He didn't do a thing about it then, and he'll not do a thing about it now." Marrying her would have stopped it. "He hasn't got a jealous bone in his body. Not for me, anyway." Not like he'd once had for Lillian.

"Do you know where the Reverend might be?" Zachariah asked.

"He's over at Kate's. Why are you asking me all these questions? Nate's gone—isn't he?"

"Not exactly."

"Then where's he heading in such a hurry?"

"The Powell ranch." He looked squarely at her. "He doesn't know."

"Doesn't know? After all this time? Where's he been? In China?"

"I reckon he's got business to tend to, so he'll be around a mite longer."

"How much of a mite longer?"

Zachariah looked down the street as though it were just a matter of time before Nate would disturb the town as much as he'd kicked up the still floating dust. "I don't know. But even another minute is longer than I'd like."

~*~

The horse's hoofs chopped up the dirt as Nate hightailed to the Powell Ranch. Nate had stumbled out of the telegraph office and into the livery where he bought a horse for twice its worth, because he didn't have time to haggle.

From afar, the Powell property looked abandoned. The cattle that had once grazed there were missing, and the grass had overtaken it. He didn't bother to take the road that led to the house. He jumped the horse over a sagging fence. The moment he reached the house, he leaped off the horse and ran to a once-grand entry, a door now scarred with chipped paint. He banged on it. "Open up!"

It should have been a servant who answered.

"Nate?"

His mother answered the door, a grayish cast to her once-fair Irish skin, and the way she fell into his arms and cried like a broken woman proved Zachariah had been right.

Marcus Powell, Nate's father, had died.

"He's been gone a year now." Nate's mother dabbed at her eyes with an embroidered handkerchief.

Nate sat across from his mother in the parlor holding her hand as she tearfully summarized the struggle. An unusually hard winter took its toll on the cattle. Snow wasn't a stranger to Ramsden, but a blizzard hard enough to kill most of the herd was a fluke. But the greatest fluke was in the irony that Marcus had enclosed his entire property with barbed wire to keep free-grazing cattle off his land, and that was the catalyst that destroyed his business. When the blizzards hit, his own cattle couldn't migrate south to escape the bitter cold, and so they froze to death. And then the failure of the business took its toll on Marcus.

Nate's mother still wore her widow's dress. Blond haired, fair skinned, slight of frame, her bones must have been made of steel because of her resiliency. But she'd lost weight and there was a pallor in her once-rosy cheeks. She'd been able to sell some of her possessions, and though she lived as meagerly as bare necessities allowed—and the looseness of her dress attested it was too meagerly—the remaining money she'd kept locked in the safe probably wasn't enough for even the poorest outlaw to bother to steal.

"I had to let go of all the help, including the house workers, and now I can't keep up with things. The house needs painting, the wallpaper is peeling, and some of the drawers have gone crooked. Our home was so lovely. I can't bear to see it this way." She paused to look at the bare walls where shadows of a grandfather clock, a rosewood wall table, and the fine carvings of a giltwood mirror had been etched into the memory of the house. "Marcus had said you were staying with Aunt Sarah, and I wrote you several times. Why didn't you write back, Nate? Didn't you get my letters?" Her eyes began to mist again.

He sat on the settee and held her to his shoulder, feeling her bones beneath the dress and the jar of her deep sobs. It was only because he'd wanted nothing to do with his father that he'd thrown her letters out. Marcus hadn't told her where Nate had really been.

"Nate?"

She roused him from that dungeon of a place back to the sunny parlor of the Powell ranch. "Yes, Mother?"

"Would you like to visit his grave?"

"How about the note on the ranch, Mother? Have you gotten any letters from the bank?"

"Several. I put them in the desk drawer." She went into Marcus's office and returned with a stack of letters. "I don't know what the bank wants. I'm sure the note has been paid." She handed the letters to Nate. "Marcus did the books after you left, and he boasted to me about how well the business was doing. So I assumed he paid off the note. He hadn't borrowed that much."

Nate's recollections of when he'd done the books agreed with what she was saying. Marcus had only borrowed five thousand dollars. With a frown, Nate slid the letter from the top envelope and started reading. Then he skimmed through another and sifted through the rest, scanning the subject line. The sun flooding the room gave way to a chill. "Mother, did you respond to any of these?"

"No," she said. "I didn't understand them. The words Mr. Tilly used were so large. I was too embarrassed to ask him what they meant, because I was afraid he would think I was a stupid woman."

"Don't call yourself stupid, Mother." Nate's face grew hot. Although it was common practice to send a perplexing letter riddled with legal and accounting jargon to a lay person, and he'd been guilty of sending them himself, he'd just never seen one of these letters from this perspective where his own dear mother was a casualty. Because Nate knew what Tilly was really after.

"But you understand the letters," his mother said, her voice now feeble with concern.

His face must have flushed with anger.

"What do they say?" she asked.

Her ashen skin, her reddened eyes, she'd had enough grief for today, and so he took in a breath of feigned lightness. "They say that when your son arrives for a visit, he should take you to town for a nice dinner and then, if you don't mind some company, he should sleep in his childhood bed, because he's as tired as Rip Van Winkle. Tomorrow I'll buy some food, and together we'll cook up a dinner we'll never forget."

She smiled, and as he kissed her on the forehead, he stared at the shadows on the wall of what she'd once had. Because what the letters said was that her embarrassment may have cost her everything.

13

The next morning, Hattie again loaded her pies onto the wagon after the same old fight with another killer chicken. But when she climbed onto the bench for the same old ride and picked up the reins and saw the gashes on her arms, something about them seemed new. Since Nate had come back, they reminded her of what really hurt.

The many proposals she'd refused from other men. The scowls she'd once gotten from pious women. The many times Boss's belt buckle cracked on her flesh. All in the hopes of hearing Nate ask her to marry him, only for him to ask another woman. Lillian.

If only Nate loved me half as much as I loved him. She rolled down her sleeves. "Giddy-up, Nellie."

Nellie clomped along for another long, bumpy ride where Hattie had nothing to do but think about her heartache. Why could she get so many men infatuated with her, but not one special man to fall in love with her? Because she was unlucky in love. Cursed in matters of the heart.

~*~

"My pa," Hattie said to her mother as Hattie pinned some socks on the clothesline. "Did he force himself on you?"

Hattie's mother was kneeling over the bucket, still scrubbing the same striped shirt collar she'd been scrubbing ten minutes ago. She'd gone at it with such vigor, it was a wonder she hadn't scrubbed the stripes off. Behind her, the wind ruffled a man's shirt and trousers hanging on the line. She gave Hattie a resigned look, because at fourteen years old, Hattie was no fool.

"No, he didn't force himself on me," she said, still scrubbing that collar.

Hattie picked up a washed shirt and whipped out some of the wrinkles. Why was it always men's dirty clothes they laundered? "Did you at least love him?"

"Don't make no never mind now, does it?"

Hattie clipped the shoulders of the shirt to the line. "It does to me."

Ever since she could remember, her mother had been scrubbing on that scrub board like the dirt would never come out. For the first time, her mother stopped scrubbing before the shirt was done. She peered into a washtub of murky water. "Yes, I loved him. I loved him like I loved no other." With earnest eyes set in her dark face, she looked up at Hattie. "You listen up, and you listen up good. You can love a man until your heart is so full of him that it feels like it's going to burst. You can even give him everything a woman can give a man. But if he's got something else in his heart, eventually it's going to shove you right out."

"What are you saying, Ma?"

"I'm saying that Powell boy you been filling your heart with is going to hurt you, and he's going to hurt you bad."

Hattie put her hands on her hips. "That ain't true."

"Ain't true, huh?" She snorted a laugh. "Only thing 'true' to those Powells is stock. He ain't never going to lower his high and mighty name to marry someone like you." She went back to scrubbing. "You keep putting your hopes in that Powell boy, and he's going to hurt you just as bad as your pa hurt me."

Hattie stopped the wagon in front of Kate's Eatery where she unloaded her pies and settled her payment. When she walked out of the eatery to head back home, she spotted the man who'd hurt her as much as her pa had hurt her ma.

~*~

Nate was just stepping off his horse when he saw Hattie coming out of Kate's Eatery on the other side of the street. He soaked in her slender profile and the poise with which she walked. She was a rare black swan that even a faded calico dress with frayed eyelet trim couldn't diminish. He imagined her in the clothes her beauty deserved, a dress draped with layers of silk and lavished with embroidery and holding a parasol with gloved hands. The black hair so plainly pulled back should be swept up and crowned with a hat adorned with bird of paradise feathers. With that image of her in mind, he smiled and tipped his hat to her.

But instead of gracing him with a nod, she stabbed him with a glare. Then she got a bucket from the wagon and filled it with water, which she brought to her old mare. As the horse drank, Hattie patted and smiled at it. If only she'd give Nate even that.

You may hate me, Hattie, but I'll never stop loving you. There was nothing he could do to repair the damage he'd done to her in the past, but he'd do his best to protect her future. He'd find a way to learn the whole truth about the Reverend and expose him.

Meanwhile, Nate had another problem to fix.

The bank was a new business in town and the

banker someone Nate had never seen before. Tilly was an elfin man who worked behind a bench too tall for him in a corner of a building that could hardly be called a bank. The only item that remotely resembled anything from a banking institution was a fine mahogany plaque inscribed with the name "Mr. Franklin Hubert Tilly." The name was bigger than the man.

"Mrs. Powell failed to apprise me that she had any living relatives, Mr. Powell, including a son," Tilly explained after Nate introduced himself. "Discerning she was a widow with no viable means, I altruistically intervened on her behalf by amending the note with an option which enabled her to remain on the property. Seeing you failed to intercede during the time allotted…" He cast an accusing glance at Nate and then folded his hands on a book splayed in front of him. Then he tilted his head back, looking down his nose and through his eyeglasses at Nate, and grinned like a tricky leprechaun. "I did my charitable duty. You *do* understand…"

"Yes, Mr. Tilly," Nate said. "I *do* understand."

Tilly glanced at the door Nate had left slightly ajar. "Then if you'll make certain to close the door on your way out…" He dismissed Nate by looking down at the book in front of him.

But Nate wasn't ready to leave. "I understand your kind of charity," Nate said. "It's the kind that preys on a widow's misfortune by exploiting her dignity in order to misappropriate her equity."

Tilly's gaze snapped back to Nate. "Your suspicions are incongruous, Mr. Powell, since she's inhabited the residence hitherto without expenditure." Having shown how long his horns were by showing how long his words were, the man arched his brow with the final say.

His ten-dollar words may have stumped other customers into submission, but Nate had a set of his own with which to lock horns.

"My accusations are apposite because the interest you mandated on my mother's so-called 'expenditures' has been exponentially excessive." He pounded onto the bench the stack of letters, seasoned with long words his mother had gotten from Tilly.

"Only because of her dereliction of payment," Tilly defended. "By rewriting, I've allowed her to stay in her house."

"At a rate of almost five times that of the conventional interest?"

Tilly fell quiet. "I admit the option was a bit...unconventional."

"Unconventional? Might we say that the only 'charity' here is that of the donations being funneled into your stockholders' pockets?" Nate looked down at the book where that information would be written. Tilly closed it, which made Nate suspect. "Or might that extra interest be going into *your* pockets?"

Tilly's face paled.

"When did you plan to evict her from her home? In nine months when the equity runs out at these outrageous payments? At which time you can sell the ranch for half its worth and still make over two thousand dollars in, shall I say, 'unrecorded interest'?"

Tilly started stammering. "Mr. Powell, I-I—"

"In case you're wondering," Nate said, "I'm a vice president at The Massachusetts National Bank. Now, are you willing to discuss another option for my mother, or shall I pursue this with the authorities?"

Tilly gulped. "I'm willing to discuss another option."

~*~

The moment Hattie heard Nate say "Good day" to Tilly, she retreated from the cracked-open door of the bank. She didn't know why she'd listened in on their conversation other than she didn't like Tilly. No one in town did. A person practically had to put up his soul as collateral to get a loan from him. She knew because she'd tried to get a small loan to buy another cook stove for her business. She climbed onto her wagon and yielded a grin. If anyone could put Tilly in his place, it was Nate. She'd always admired him for his intelligence.

Just then, Nate mounted his horse and spotted her looking at him—and worse, smiling at him.

She dropped her smile and snapped the reins. "Giddy-up, Nellie."

~*~

Hattie rode away in her wagon.

If you could stand behind my eyes for just a moment, you'd understand how much I love you. Despite what everything looked like—the unaccounted years Nate had been away—she'd know how much he'd always loved her.

Because she'd know why.

As he watched her disappear, he recalled what his heart never forgot.

"Get me a whiskey," a stranger demanded of the

bartender.

Nate thought the customer already had too many, and he didn't like the way the man was eyeing Hattie. In that old, smoky saloon packed with grubby men, she stood out like a ruby in a crate of coal.

"I haven't seen you put a penny down," the bartender said to the stranger. "Pay up first."

"Not until you set some real whiskey in front of me."

"I just gave you one," the bartender said. "What do you think that was?"

"It tasted like water out of the horse trough." The man pulled out a gun, and the place went quiet. "Now get me some real whiskey."

Judging by the man's unsteadiness, the whisky was real. Judging by the man's size, he probably thought he could get free drinks. But no man was too big and tough to handle for hard-as-nails Hattie Brown. In no time, she was by the stranger's side and whispering in his ear.

Nate stood up. If the gun turned in her direction, he would draw the stranger's attention and take the bullet if he had to.

But Hattie had things under control. She always had things under control.

The stranger grinned, liking whatever magic she was pouring into his ear. She placed her hand on his shoulder and slid it down his arm. A blink of an eye later, the gun was in Hattie's hand, aimed between the stranger's eyes. "Get out of here," she growled.

The man looked at those wildcat eyes, sobered up, and then walked out the door.

Later that same night, it was Nate she had to control. He'd gotten himself drunk and started to relive the worst day of his life. The day he'd failed to save his younger sister from the fire that killed her.

"I'm sorry, Sally. I'm sorry."

Just when he'd started to make a crying fool of himself, Hattie said to him in her soothing voice, "Why don't you lie down for a spell, Nate?"

She led him stumbling up the stairs to her bedroom. Just as he'd done many nights before, he spent the whole night in her bed, while she spent it sitting in a chair beside him, stroking his sweat-dampened hair from his forehead with her soft touch — and keeping him from getting up and killing Zachariah.

A rickety sound interrupted Nate from his thoughts.

A stagecoach was coming down the road.

Zachariah stepped out of the sheriff's office onto the walk where he stood with his arms akimbo. Stagecoaches had always been a rare sight because Ramsden was a throughway to nowhere and a destination to nothing.

Except it contained Hattie, so in that respect, Ramsden had everything.

The stagecoach pulled up to the saloon and left behind a man who looked as if he'd gotten off in the wrong town. He was an older fellow with white hair, a white cutaway jacket, and splatter-dashes. He took a few hesitant steps looking for something but not knowing where to start. "Excuse me, sir." He raised a hand, flagging a man he had something in common with: a three-piece suit. But the suit Nate was wearing wasn't as fine as this man's. This man wore the apparel of a true gentleman.

The details of his satin lapel, the scrolled silver handle on his cane, and an engraved gold chain watch he consulted as he approached Nate revealed the gentleman was not only a man of means—but of considerable means.

"I say, excuse me. I'm looking for someone." His Georgian accent divulged he'd come a long way looking for that someone.

Nate couldn't help but snicker. "Are you sure you have the right town?"

"This is Ramsden, isn't it?"

"It is."

"I'm looking for a woman."

"Aren't we all?" Nate laughed lightly. "If you're looking for a woman, Ramsden is the wrong place to find one. There aren't many around."

The man chuckled. "No, you don't understand, sir. You see, I'm looking for one woman in particular. I understand she lives here in Ramsden."

Nate knew of no woman who had anything in common with a man like this. Perhaps she was someone who'd moved in while he was away. But why would such a significant woman move to such an insignificant town? "She must be very 'particular' indeed."

"Indeed she is," the gentleman said. "Perhaps you may know her. Her name is Miss Henrietta Brown."

Nate's blood stopped pumping. He'd heard that name only once before, and long ago at that, because the woman was better known by another name.

Hattie?

14

What could a Southern gentleman possibly want with Hattie?

Zachariah was keeping a close eye on him and the stranger.

Nate feigned a cordial smile. "If you don't mind me asking, what would a man like you want from a woman from a place like this?"

"It's a matter of a personal nature," the gentleman said. "You understand."

Nate understood what *"a personal nature"* between a beautiful woman and a rich man twice her age could mean. From beau to benevolence to blackmail. "I'm sorry, I can't help you." He nodded toward Zachariah. "But you might try the sheriff." Nate could have choked on his own words, but Zachariah would have Hattie's best interests in mind.

There were now two men in Hattie's life. They appeared to have nothing in common—aside from their interest in Hattie.

The gentleman appeared to be mild-mannered enough—but then again, so did the Reverend. Nate could only handle the matter he'd already set his mind on, the Reverend. Evidence. He needed something to shove in front of Zachariah's face so he'd arrest him. And Nate would look for that something while the Reverend was conducting Sunday service.

***

"'It is well, it is well with my soul.'"

Sunlight poured through the windows of the church. The pews were full, and the voices almost drowned out the fine music Lillian was playing on the piano.

Although the words of a hymn about peace and assurance came out of Hattie's mouth, her mind was more on the lines of fang and claw.

She couldn't deny that Nate's return had awakened her yearning to marry him. All her praying hadn't made her feelings for him go away. *With Nate being so close, I'm fighting every minute from wanting to run to him, so...what do I do, Lord?* She'd grown comfortable being alone, because he was the only man she'd ever wanted. *Maybe if I put my all into falling in love with a Godly man ... someone I can trust to be faithful...* then maybe God would help her with the rest by helping her forget Nate.

There were only two eligible bachelors—Clayton and the Reverend. Clayton, being twenty years older, left her with only one option. She'd have to sink her fangs and claws into the Reverend. Those weren't comely thoughts for a Christian woman. Besides, didn't everyone in town think she and the Reverend should get married?

Her prey stood behind the pulpit, singing with vigor, his mouth wide and his eyeglasses halfway down his nose. *He's not exactly what a woman would deem the knight-in-shining-armor type, Lord, but there's got to be something savory about him—if You'd please accommodate by showing me what it is.*

He's a lanky kind of tall and a gangly kind of slim.

No, that didn't whet her appetite. *Let's look for something else, Lord.*

Hair. He had a nice thick head of dark brown hair—*if he'd just part it on the side instead of in the middle so his cowlick wouldn't stand straight up dead center on his crown like the tail of a surprised coonhound.*

It was impossible to be attracted to him after seeing Nate. So...*maybe I'm approaching this all wrong. Maybe the trick is to make myself less attracted to Nate...* She glanced from the Reverend to Lillian, up front, playing the piano. Lillian was a pretty little thing, soft-spoken and refined, a real lady straight from England. In fact, with a set of wings on her back she could have been a fairy princess. She and Nate would have looked fine together, and apparently Nate thought so too, since she was the woman he'd gotten engaged to instead of Hattie.

Her blood started boiling with righteous anger. She didn't want to hate Nate, she just wanted to be good and mad at him, and so she turned up the fire by imagining Lillian and Nate holding hands. The anger rose from her toes to her torso, and when she could taste it on her tongue, she looked back at the Reverend, and smiled. *That did the trick, Lord. The Reverend does look a bit tastier.*

Or at least, a little less sour.

~*~

What are you hiding, Reverend?

Nate squatted beneath a window. He'd waited for everyone to pour into the church, including his mother, Zachariah and his family, and Hattie. Finally, the door had closed, and as they sang the opening hymn, Nate slipped around the back to the parsonage.

He tried the door. Locked. He tried a window. It wouldn't budge. He tried another. *No one bolts up their houses, not in this quiet town.* The Reverend was definitely hiding something.

"'Whatever my lot…'"

Nate had an opportunity to make some noise before the song ended. He wrapped his coat around a rock to mute the crash, and broke a window. Had anyone heard? His question was answered with the refrain.

"'It is well…'"

He kicked out the shards, climbed in and landed beside the stove. The kitchen consisted of a simple square table with two chairs neatly tucked beneath, and a wall of shelves. The top shelf held canned goods lined up according to contents. The second shelf held a rack displaying four dishes with a blue floral design and four matching cups, all with their handles facing right. The third shelf held one pot and two pans. A sack of flour and a sack of beans sat on a clean floor. The man epitomized the expression "Cleanliness is next to Godliness." It was tidy—but offered no good place to hide something.

What exactly did Nate expect to find?

Two doors led off the kitchen. One door was left opened, and the other was closed. He gripped the handle of the closed door.

Another meticulously clean room. A neatly-made bed, clothes buttoned and hung on pegs, and a dresser draped with a doily. Nate ran his finger over the dresser. *Not even a speck of dust.* He opened a drawer to find a row of folded socks. He'd never seen a man—or a woman for that matter—this neat.

If he touched anything, the Reverend would know someone had been here. But with the window broken and glass on the floor…

Nate rummaged through socks and folded shirts in drawer after drawer, tossing the contents. *Only clothes.* He pushed the dresser to see if something might be hidden beneath. *Not even dust.*

"'It is well…'" The song rang out as though the clever Reverend mocked him.

The hymn ended, but Nate wouldn't abandon his quest. *I know it's in here, and I'm going to find it.*

The only other room housed a walnut bookcase and a desk. A typical preacher's office. On top of the desk lay a closed, leather-bound Bible, the spine a little frayed from use. A fountain pen rested in its stand beside a closed ink jar. Centered on the desk, slightly tilted, a piece of paper listed several Bible verses written out with the skill of a calligrapher.

Nate searched through the desk drawers but only found a pile of sermons stacked in alphabetical order. He snatched a latched box. Could this be where that *something* was hidden? He unhooked the latch and peeled back the hinged lid.

A spare ink bottle.

I'm getting nowhere. The Reverend's secret is hidden somewhere within reach—but where? Think.

Except for the damage Nate had done, nothing was out of place.

In fact, the Reverend was overly neat. Excessively organized. Exaggeratedly deliberate.

Another old adage came to mind and kept repeating itself. *A place for everything, and everything in its place.* Whatever gave the Reverend away wasn't hidden—it was properly organized. *So how does one organize where to put something one wants to hide?*

Nate rubbed his jaw. *A man can't let go of his past.* Hattie was Nate's proof of that. *You always come back to it. So what do you keep coming back to, Reverend?* Nate panned the room until his gaze settled on the bookcase. However, instead of recklessly tossing the books off the shelves, he carefully read the spine of the books.

The Pilgrim's Progress. Ben-Hur: A Tale of the Christ. Bonifacius (Essays to Do Good). God's Mercy Surmounting Man's Cruelty. Book of Common Prayer. Hymnal. Sermons by John Wesley. Sinners in the Hands of an Angry God. The Good Old—

He looked back at the previous book.

Sinners in the Hands of an Angry God.

He plucked the tome off the shelf. The book split open of its own accord and surrendered a piece of paper. Folded, yellowed, worn to the point it tore in the creases—it was exactly what Nate was looking for.

A faded "Wanted Dead or Alive" poster submitted four sketched faces, among them the Reverend's likeness, and underneath it the name Jacob "Jake" Cadwell. The caption on the poster read, "Krugar Gang."

Nate's knees buckled with the memory of the night he'd run into the gang on his way into Ramsden. The elusive leader of this notorious gang had never stepped out of the shadows but Nate knew his name, Joe Krugar. *Hattie's bumbling beau belongs to a gang of cold-blooded killers.* And Nate was the one who'd advertised for a clergyman and recklessly hired a wanted man.

Nate noted two discrepancies between the poster in his hand and the ones he'd seen posted all over Kansas. The first discrepancy was in the amount of the reward. The poster on the train offered four thousand dollars. This one offered only two thousand. The smaller reward and well-worn folds suggested it was older. The second discrepancy was the number of gang members. This named five. The poster on the train named four. The man missing was the Reverend. *Why?*

It seemed the Reverend was even more mysterious than Joe Krugar.

~*~

When the hymn ended, Hattie sat down. No breeze came through the open windows, and so she fanned herself with her hymnal.

The Reverend tapped his sermon into a neat stack. The pulpit was too short for him and he had to hunch forward to read. It wasn't the most handsome posture, but one she decided to attribute to a more attractive trait—intelligence. Why did she think intelligence was so handsome? Because Nate was so smart. She fanned with the determination to get over him. *Lord, even if You can help me fall in love with the Reverend, how am I going to get him to fall in love with me?*

Although he'd come around to offer his help, he never came courting. He talked a lot, but nothing romantic. Slow would be the best way to describe him, since it'd been seven whole years since they'd first met. Not that she'd done much to encourage him. But now that the matter came up... *What's he waiting for? An angel to smack him over the head and say, "Start courting the woman before she dies of old age, for Pete's sake"?* If a man's piety was measured by his awkwardness around a woman, then the Reverend was as pious as they came. The Lord had to be behind her all the way on this. *It's time to yank this acquaintance up a notch.*

Just as the Reverend took a sip from a glass of water to clear his throat, he suddenly got butter-fingered. The water glass leaped above his head, and then started coming down. He caught the glass, but as he fumbled to hold onto it, water splashed all over. He groped, the glass slipped. He grabbed, it slid.

Everyone sat paralyzed, watching helplessly.

It was a fight to the very end—when the Reverend caught the glass an inch from disaster.

A deacon gingerly took the glass from the Reverend's hand.

Everyone applauded the miracle that the glass didn't break.

The fight had taken its toll on the Reverend. His shoulders and hair were wet, and his eyeglasses, out of kilter across his face, were splayed with droplets. But the Reverend survived and so did the glass. Something else, however, didn't make it. He peeled the limp mess of papers off his pulpit.

"I'm afraid I...I suppose I could...excuse me... I have notes... I'll just get them." He pointed toward the parsonage and left.

It was times like this that erased all Hattie's suspicions that the Reverend could be anything other than a bungler. She snorted. *And Nate thinks you're a crack shot.*

~*~

Nate stood in the parsonage speculating about the Reverend's current standing with the law. Had he been left out of the current "Wanted Dead or Alive" poster because the authorities thought he was dead? If that was so, then it was no wonder the man could hide in plain sight. And what better disguise than a white collar?

Was he still involved with the gang? An informant or watchman, perhaps? Or maybe *he* was the leader. Was Joe Krugar even real?

But Nate distinctly remembered the figure he'd seen that night of a small man. *Is that why I encountered the gang? Are they coming to Ramsden looking for the Reverend?* That raised even more questions. *This isn't a good place to stand around and think.* It was time to leave. But when he turned to do just that, the door creaked.

"Nate Powell," the Reverend said. "I thought that might be you."

15

Nate drew his gun, but the Reverend was as calm as a baby in his nanny's arms.

"Tell me something," the Reverend said. "Do you make it a habit of sneaking around?"

"No less than you—Cadwell."

Cadwell's gaze lowered to the poster in Nate's hand.

"Family picture?"

"I wish you hadn't found that." Cadwell took a step closer.

Nate raised his gun.

Cadwell held up his hands. "You know, Nate, I've got a church full of people waiting on me."

"You mean, a church full of people waiting on someone you're *not*."

Cadwell's calmness made it clear he'd been in similar predicaments before—and his freedom attested he'd gotten himself out of them. "I'd say if a man's holding a gun, he'd better use it."

"I don't need to shoot you. Not when I've got something better." Nate glanced at the poster.

Cadwell lunged, twisted his hand, and before Nate could blink, Cadwell was holding the gun. He flipped the pistol.

Nate stood eye to eye with the barrel of his own gun. "I'd say if a man's holding a gun, he'd better use it." Nate challenged.

"And I'd say, I don't need to shoot you, either. Not when *I've* got something better." Cadwell nodded toward the wall. "I've got half the town and the sheriff in that room. Imagine what would happen if I called for help. Who do you think the sheriff'll listen to? The outcast standing in the broken glass from the window he smashed, or the man who's been preaching to them for years? I don't know everything about you, Nate, but seeing you sneaking into town the other day told me everything I need to know."

Nate's jaw tensed.

The Reverend nudged the gun barrel toward the desk. "Now, put the poster in the drawer."

Nate had no choice. "I don't care who you are, so long as you steer clear of Hattie. You can take that as a warning."

Cadwell fired the gun.

Nate put a hand to his throat where the bullet breezed by, and a finger through a hole in his necktie. He swallowed. If ever there was a crack shot, that was it.

"And you can take that as a warning to stay clear of me," Cadwell said.

There was a ruckus outside as everyone in the church came running.

Zachariah got to the door first. "What's going on here?" The look in his eyes after he glanced at the broken glass and then at Nate was enough to tell Nate he was going to the jailhouse.

But for some reason, Cadwell headed it off. "Nate was just walking up to the church when I spotted his fine revolver and asked to see it. I'm afraid that when he handed it over to me, my finger got caught in the trigger, and...." His glance at the broken window finished the tale. Then, using a lot less grace than when he'd snatched it, he feigned almost dropping the gun as he offered it back to Nate.

Nate holstered the gun, knowing fully well if he drew it on Cadwell, Zachariah and every man there would draw their guns on him.

With or without a weapon, Cadwell had the upper hand. He fished some papers from the same drawer he'd made Nate put the poster in and closed the drawer slowly, as if to emphasize his advantage. Then he planted a firm hand on Nate's shoulder. "I'm glad you could join us for church."

~*~

"'Though I speak with the tongues of men and of angels, and have not charity, I am become as sounding brass, or a tinkling cymbal.'" Hattie watched the Reverend's glasses slide down his nose as he read from the Bible on his too-low pulpit.

Everyone had settled back in church, except for her. With Nate having joined them, she was thoroughly unsettled.

"'And though I have the gift of prophecy, and understand all mysteries, and all knowledge; and though I have all faith, so that I could remove mountains—'"

At the moment, moving mountains specifically referred to removing Nate, who was sitting in her line of sight, albeit not on purpose. He'd simply sat by his mother's side after escorting her to her pew, seating her, and helping straighten her shawl. Watching him treat his mother so tenderly irritated Hattie, because Nate was such a gentleman.

"'Charity suffereth long, and is kind...'"

Hattie's gaze kept shifting from Nate's perfect head of wavy blond hair to the Reverend's cowlick just beyond. Why was that one sprig of hair all she saw when she looked at him?

"'...Beareth all things, believeth all things, hopeth all things, endureth all things...'"

Beareth. Believeth. Hopeth. Endureth. Those words summarized a sermon that seemed to last for days with Nate being so near and demanding every ounce of perseverance. She found herself paying more attention to him than she was to the Reverend, until her mind started to drift, and to the most ungodly of places.

"Get me a whiskey, Hattie."

"Hey, Hattie, come on over here."

The place was packed, but she knew which men to play. She shouted to the bartender, "Fetch these men a drink." Then she slung her arm over one old coot's shoulder and put her mouth to his ear. He smelled as if he'd wrestled with a skunk.

She breathed into the man's ear, "Tell you what, Clyde." She had no idea what his real name was, nor did she care. She just called him Clyde because they were all the same. Groping, burping, dirty men with a little bit of money that Boss wanted. "Let's you and me make a bet."

"What you got to offer me?" he said with a look that raked her from the lowcut neckline of her red dress to her rouge-painted lips.

"Hey fellers," Hattie called out. "I want to place a bet with Clyde here. Think I got something he wants?"

Her question was answered by whoops and hollers.

"How about one big, sloppy kiss?" she said to Clyde.

His eyes lit up.

"I'll set you up for—" she was going to say four, but figured she could rustle him for six more drinks. "A half-dozen shots. If you belt all of them down by the time I count to twenty, I'll kiss you like you ain't never been kissed before."

It was a chance for him to prove his manhood, and he pounded his money down. She fetched the whiskies and placed them in front of him. "Ready, Clyde?" she called out.

"I'm ready," he called back with gall, as though he'd already won.

"He's ready, boys," she announced, and more whooping and hollering followed. When she started to count, the men joined in. Clyde was so drunk before he started, that in three drinks, he was flat out on the floor.

She'd played this game many a time and never lost a one. She always made sure the odds were in her favor, because there was only one man she saved her kisses for. Nate sat at his usual table, watching her, nothing else. Why couldn't he get even a little jealous over her?

"'But when that which is perfect is come, then that which is in part shall be done away…'"

When Hattie's mind came back to church, she discovered that not only was she looking at Nate, but that he was looking at her.

Angry that he'd caught her looking, she pulled her gaze away and set it on the cowlick. Rather, the Reverend. She forced herself to smile.

~*~

Nate shook his head with regret. There was a time Hattie used to smile at him that way, and he wished she still did.

Her, Cadwell, church, they all added up to an uncomfortable place to be. Especially since he surmised Cadwell had put Nate there to keep an eye on him.

"'For now we see through a glass, darkly; but then face to face: now I know in part; but then shall I know even as also I am known.'" Even the sermon had a double meaning—because Cadwell was preaching it.

Nate's mother started cooling herself with a mother-of-pearl hand fan.

"Are you all right, Mother?" Nate whispered. She looked pale. She'd been through a lot, and he regretted staying away so long and making her go through the worst alone.

"I'm just warm," she said.

"Let me help you off with your shawl." As Nate lifted it off her shoulders, he spotted old acquaintances now married to mail-order brides they'd sent for from England before he'd gone away.

Lillian was one of them. Though she was pretty, she was no Hattie. Lillian was simply an opportunity to humiliate Zachariah, who'd sent for her but was too scared to claim her. So Nate claimed her with the intention of raising her hopes that she would marry him. Nate's plan was to throw her back at Zachariah so he could see her getting an eyeful of the man she would really marry. Scars and all.

But Lillian failed to play her part. She never fell for Nate. Things escalated out of control, and she turned out to be the battleground for a full-score revenge that had evolved into her life for Sally's. *Sally.* The memory of his late sister was a dangerous place for his mind to visit. A place he didn't want to get lost in. He pulled himself out.

Lillian, now in the fullness of motherhood, came back into view. She must have seen beyond the scars because she looked happy by Zachariah's side. Next to her was the second prettiest little girl Nate had ever seen.

No girl could be as pretty as the one who'd once shined even in a burlap dress. He caught himself smiling at that memory of Hattie. Then he caught Hattie glaring at him and realized his gaze had been cast in Lillian's direction.

Hattie averted her gaze, reminding Nate of his arrogance and how circumstances had backfired a hundredfold because he'd lost what he'd wanted most. Her.

Revenge. It was an ugly thing to think about in church. But then again, having a member of the Krugar Gang for a preacher invalidated the sanctity of the service.

16

"Nate, it's good to see you back in town," Doctor Hinkle said after service. "It's been a long time."

While his mother visited with a group of women, old acquaintances came over to shake Nate's hand.

It was a sunny day on the church grounds, the sky was clearer than the ones he'd become accustomed to back East. Boston skies were always cloudy.

"Are you here to stay?" Doctor Hinkle asked.

"Just long enough to take care of some business." As he eyed Cadwell, Nate's answer had a dual meaning. If ever there was a wolf in sheep's clothing, it was standing there acting like a pious clown. Cadwell had Hattie fooled. He had the whole town fooled. If Nate hadn't stumbled upon him practicing with his gun, he'd have likely had Nate fooled as well.

"I'm sorry to hear your mother is losing her home," Doctor Hinkle's wife, Prudence, said. "It's a good thing you came back to help her."

Nate followed her glare to where Tilly, the banker, stood.

Knowing everyone else's business in a small town wasn't necessarily a bad thing. Especially when someone could offer a solution.

"I have an elderly patient who will be moving in with family shortly," Doctor Hinkle said. "Her cabin will be up for sale. It might suit your mother well."

Nate had tried to convince his mother to move to

Massachusetts, but she'd refused to leave Ramsden. Meanwhile, he had yet to see the money Tilly had promised. Still, Nate would ensure his mother was cared for, even if he had to dig into his own pockets. "Any idea how much they'd want for it?"

"I don't think it'd be too much," Doctor Hinkle said. "It's a small place, but nice enough."

Something captured Prudence's attention. "I could never see those two together."

Doctor Hinkle shook his head. "I think they can't either, which is likely why they still aren't married after all this time. I always thought it would be you and Hattie, Nate."

Cadwell was playing his game again, clumsily helping Hattie onto her wagon. When he climbed up beside her, Nate abruptly excused himself and ran over.

"Don't go with him," he said to Hattie. The warning that Cadwell was part of a murdering gang caught in Nate's throat.

Cadwell's unworried smile reminded Nate that he was the outsider and the Reverend the trusted citizen.

"Look here, Nate," Hattie said. "I've gone on with my life. Now get on with yours."

Though Cadwell very well knew the answer, he feigned bewilderment. "Are you and he...?" With his hair slicked down and parted in the middle—and a cowlick standing straight up—he looked to be ten times the fool he wasn't.

Hattie glared Nate down as she answered Cadwell. "We were, but not anymore."

"Then I reckon you have no business bothering these two."

The hair rose on the back of Nate's neck as

Zachariah came up from behind him.

The comfortable grin on Cadwell's face confirmed that if there would be any trouble, it would be Nate going to the jailhouse.

Nate reluctantly backed away from Hattie's wagon—and Zachariah standing as their protector. Protector indeed. Had Zachariah at least found out what that Southern gentleman wanted with Hattie?

This wasn't the time or place to find out.

~*~

In Hattie's desperate attempt to get her mind off Nate she'd invited the Reverend over for Sunday dinner. Maybe a cozy meal together would lead to a conversation where they could learn something about one another that would spark some interest.

Nellie wasn't getting any younger; the ride was slow and bumpy and the wagon wheels creaked. The Reverend insisted on taking the horse's reins, and Hattie relented and then regretted it, because putting anything in the man's hands turned something harmless into a hazard. She hoped the Reverend wouldn't cause the old mare to break into a run and race the rest of her life out of her. *Gingerly. Please treat the old gal gingerly.*

"Tell me about your history with Nate," the Reverend said.

"We liked one another once."

"He still seems fond of you."

That was odd. The Reverend was giving her that "something's not quite right" feeling about him again. She'd known the Reverend to be slow to catch on most of the time. So why had he latched on to her and Nate's feelings for one another all of a sudden?

"It takes two, and I'm not interested. Don't worry about Nate. He'll be gone as soon as his business with his mother is done." That last sentence came out with a silent groan from her heart.

"Are you sure you're not his primary business here?" The Reverend's gaze met Hattie's for a moment.

His cowlick suddenly didn't look as silly. In fact, at that moment, she might have mistaken him for downright astute. That moment, however, was cut short. Nellie had come to a standstill. Was the old gal finally giving out? Hattie was about to leap out of the wagon to check on the mare, when she noticed something. "You're leaning on the break handle, Reverend." She tried not to be irritated at the fright he'd given her.

"Oh...I..."

Astute? The Reverend was still the most oblivious man she'd ever met.

Sitting across from the Reverend at the dining table was like having Sunday dinner with a cowlick. The Reverend felt all wrong for her, and her mind kept slipping to how she wished she were looking into blue eyes in a handsome face framed by light, wavy hair, and talking about love that made her feel all warm inside. Instead, they were talking about her cooking.

"I've had your chicken pies at Kate's," he said. "Your chicken and dumplings are even more delicious." He sat as stiff and upright as his cowlick while he ate.

Her gaze slid to the glasses slipping down his nose. "I just wish chicken grew in the ground like potatoes and were just as passive to prepare," she muttered. How she wished he were Nate. The only thing Hattie learned about the Reverend was to never let him help with the dishes.

The man was so clumsy it was a wonder he managed to stay alive. He must have had a dozen guardian angels scurrying around him, moving this in his way to catch whatever fell, and that out of his way to prevent a calamity. It was one near disaster after another. The man couldn't move without almost creating a mishap. Those angels must have been grateful for the peace when he finally fell asleep at the end of the day. She could picture the lot of them sitting around his bed, shoulders slumped, feathers haggard, and dead tired—which was how she felt after she'd finally dropped him off at the parsonage.

When she headed back home, her heart pounded as slowly as Nellie's gait as she tried to get her mind off Nate.

17

Monday morning Nate had two things on his agenda. The first was to go see Tilly and look into the money due his mother.

"I'm still working on it." Tilly fidgeted. "These things take time."

Apparently, Tilly had already spent the money he'd "neglected" to put on the books.

Nate knew how to hurry him along. "So I assume you'll extend the time my mother has before she has to leave the ranch?"

Tilly's narrow jaw dropped. "But we agreed on one month. I have a buyer."

"We also agreed on the money," Nate said. "So I suggest you take less time getting it, so she can take less time moving out."

Now to tend to the second thing on his agenda.

Finding out what that Southern gentleman wanted with Hattie wouldn't come as easily, especially since Zachariah was the one he'd have to ask. Nate stepped out onto the walk.

Hattie stopped her wagon in front of Kate's and started bringing pies into the eatery.

Maybe if he helped her it would patch things up between them. He picked two pies out of the wagon.

She came out and stopped short at the sight of him.

"Hello, Hattie."

She snatched the pies from him. "Good-bye, Nate." She turned her back and stormed toward the eatery.

"It seems every conversation I try to have with you ends up with you, in essence, telling me to go back to wherever I came from."

"And you're just figuring that out now?" She asked over her shoulder.

Zachariah crossed the street. "I'll help you in a minute, Hattie."

"Thank you, Zachariah." She disappeared inside the eatery.

Knowing the business Zachariah would first want to take care of was getting rid of him, Nate took the opportunity to ask a question. "Did a man come to see you about Hattie?"

Zachariah eyed him. "You sent him?"

"Yes, I did."

"So you figure whatever he wants with her is your business."

Nate's faced heated. Zachariah had headed him off.

"Hattie *is* my business," Nate said. "You act as though I'm a threat to her. I would never hurt a hair on her head."

Zachariah crossed his arms in response, or lack thereof.

"And meanwhile," Nate responded. "You're leaving her at the mercy of an outlaw who's as dangerous as they come—and he's right under your nose."

"You wouldn't happen to be talking about the Reverend again now, would you?" He eyed Nate with a guarded expression.

Zachariah was mistrustful of the wrong person.

"That man's as much of a reverend as I am. His name is Jacob Cadwell, and he's the best gunman I've ever seen. He's lying to Hattie. He's lying to everyone here. That butter-finger bumbling of his is all an act—and you're a blind fool not to see through it."

"So, what exactly is he lying about?" Zachariah's voice, flat with indifference, suggested it was Nate who needed to be set straight.

Nate stepped toward Zachariah. The man, a head taller, looked even bigger this close. Determined to make Zachariah listen for Hattie's sake, Nate stood his ground. "What he's been hiding from you for the past seven years, *Sheriff*," he mocked, "is that he's a part of the Krugar Gang. In case you don't know about them, they're a band of cold-blooded murderers. If you contact the authorities in Kansas City—"

"I've got a picture of the gang I've been staring at for a year hanging in my office, so I know well enough who they are." Zachariah added with a growl in his voice as he looked down at Nate, "And I know who they are *not*."

"The Reverend isn't on that poster; he's on an older one, and he's got one of those in the parsonage. He hid it in the—"

"So you *did* break in."

Zachariah had missed the whole point, fraying Nate's patience with him. "Since you were too thick-headed to even look into what I told you about the Reverend and his shooting skills, I needed some kind of evidence—"

"If you go near the Reverend again," Zachariah growled, "I will lock you up."

"Lock *me* up? If you were doing your job, I

wouldn't have to do it for you."

"I *am* doing my job."

Nate's patience had frayed down to the last string, but fortunately this was a string of sensibility. Even if Zachariah didn't know about Nate's attempt to kill Lillian, he knew that Nate had tried to marry her out from under him. "I admit I haven't exactly been a saint in the past, but I'm not the one you need to worry about now. The man you take to be a saint is the one you need to worry about. I'll show you." Nate urged, "I'll take you to where he practices his shooting so you can see–"

"You're not hearing me." Zachariah raised his voice. "What I want to see is you staying away from the Reverend."

Nate, in turn, raised his voice. "No, Zachariah, you're not hearing me. The man is dangerous. I'm trying to protect Hattie."

"*I'll* protect Hattie." And Zachariah's glare made it clear that Nate was the one Zachariah was protecting her from.

The badge that had once made old Sheriff Breck open-minded had made Sheriff Zachariah Keane obstinate. Nate clenched his jaw against reminding Zachariah he'd once been nothing but a hired hand on his family's ranch. His jaw clenched harder with a reminder to himself that Zachariah had won Nate's father's favor and his sister's fancy—and now the whole town's approval by being their sheriff.

"Now," Zachariah pressed." When will you be finished with your business here in Ramsden?"

Had it not been for that emblem shining off Zachariah's vest, Nate wouldn't have spat out his answer so politely. "You'll have to ask your banker that, because I'm waiting on the money he agreed to pay my mother." Her problem served as a good excuse to stick around, and Zachariah knew it, because he didn't say a word in protest.

When Hattie finally came out of the eatery, Nate tipped his hat to her. "I see you already have help. Good day, Hattie." After an eye-to-eye glare with Zachariah, he left.

~*~

Hattie tried not to watch Nate leave, because every time she did, she yearned to go with him.

"How are you doing?" Unlike the Reverend, Zachariah was insightful enough to know when her heart ached.

"I'll be doing better once he's gone."

With an unreadable look on his face, Zachariah watched Nate as if he knew something about him but wasn't telling her. "The Reverend's a fine man, Hattie."

She appreciated his attempt to get her mind off Nate, but in that respect, Zachariah wasn't insightful at all. He was wishful. As wishful as she'd been. *The Reverend just isn't right for me, Lord.* She wanted to say that to Zachariah as her gaze stayed on the only man who was right for her.

Nate got onto his horse and rode out of sight, along with her heart.

After bringing the rest of her pies into Kate's, Zachariah said, "I reckon there ain't going to be a right time to tell you this."

"Tell me what?" Hattie said.

"There's a man looking for you."

She snorted. Back when she'd worked in the

saloon, many a man just passing through had come through again to ask her to marry him. She waved her hand dismissingly. "I don't want to know about it."

"You might want to know about this man."

She crossed her arms. Couldn't Zachariah see she already had enough on her mind? "And why is that?"

Zachariah paused. "Because the man claims to be your pa."

Her fingers tightened around the pie basket. No man had ever claimed that. But she could solve this predicament easily enough. "Did he give you a name?"

"Mr. Jonathan Parker. Says he's from Georgia."

Her numbness turned to weakness.

"Who's my pa?"

Hattie rarely saw her mother other than over a bucket and a washboard. She looked tired beyond her years, and she scrubbed just as listlessly as if she were doing it in her sleep.

"He was my master's son," she surrendered. It seemed all the scrubbing had finally taken the fight out of her.

"I didn't know you were a slave, Ma."

"I was born a slave. Never knew my own pa. Never wanted to have a child who didn't." She stopped scrubbing and looked down into the water as if she saw something in there. "I met your pa when I was fourteen years old. Me and my sister, we was up for auction, and two men bid on us. The first one, he had me scared stiff as a broomstick the way he kept looking at me. The second, well, that was your grandpa, and he was as Christian a man as I suppose they come, because he rescued me, Hattie. He rescued me and my sister from a man known for beating his slaves.

"The master's son, he took a shining to me, and I took a shining to him, and then it just happened that we done what we shouldn't ought to have done. I knowed it was wrong.

And I knowed it was even more wrong, but when I started to feel a baby growing inside me, I was so scared of getting caught in my sin that I stole money from the master's house. That's how I paid my way here." She hesitated. *"This is the first time I ever told anybody that. I never even told my sister."* She looked into the wash bucket, with longing in her eyes.

"You miss your sister, Ma?" Hattie said softly.

Her mother yielded a rare smile. *"Her name was Hattie. That's where your name come from."* She wiped some mist from her eyes. *"And I'm going to tell you something else I ain't never told nobody, neither. Jonathan. That was your pa's name. Jonathan Garrison Parker."*

"Hattie," Zachariah said. "Are you all right?"

No, she wasn't. First Nate...and now this? But Zachariah had a family and a whole town to care for. She'd already loaded enough trouble on him with Nate being back because of her. "I'll be fine," she said. Maybe not for the moment, but with the Lord's healing, eventually she'd be.

"Mr. Parker wants to talk with you. He's staying at the hotel."

She stared at the brick building with the swinging doors. The only hotel in town was the one over the saloon where Boss had kept her prisoner. She wouldn't set foot near that place, let alone in it. Staring at the saloon changed her weakness into indignation. That place and everyone in it had brought her nothing but grief. Including her pa. "You can tell Mr. Parker not to bother waiting around." She climbed onto her wagon. "Thank you for your help, Zachariah."

~*~

Nate hid himself behind a sagging barn as he waited for Hattie to arrive home. Every minute she spent with Cadwell was a minute she was in danger. If Zachariah couldn't see that, Nate would do his utmost to make sure she did. He'd tell her about Cadwell, but he'd first make her a promise—a promise he'd have to force himself to keep.

Finally, her slow-as-molasses mare came into sight. As she unhitched her horse and watered it, he wished she'd render him half the affection she gave the old horse. She spotted him and closed the door before he could follow her into the house.

He knocked. "Hattie, open up." He knocked again. "There's something I have to tell you. Hattie, please."

"What part of 'Don't bother me' doesn't sink in, Nate?" She was listening.

He called through the door, "There's something important I have to tell you." He hesitated before adding, "If you'll just listen to me this one last time, I promise it's the last thing I'll ever say to you."

"I've already listened to you enough. What more can you tell me?"

"It's not about us."

"Then who's it about?"

"It's about the Reverend. You can't go near the man, Hattie. He's dangerous."

She threw open the door. "I know. You think he's a bumbling fool."

"It's worse than that. The man's lying to you. He's lying to everyone."

"*He's* lying?" She put a hand on the cotton fabric that skimmed over her waist, cinching it in and revealing the shapely figure beneath. "So what's *he* lying about?"

"His clumsiness, Hattie. It's all an act."

She paused.

"Come on, Hattie, you're no dupe. You've got to suspect something's not right about the man."

Her brow furrowed. "Like what...exactly?"

"He's the best gunman I've ever seen. I caught him practicing out in the wilds."

"So—why would he be acting like someone he isn't?"

"Because he's a member of the Krugar Gang."

"You mean that band of outlaws on the poster hanging in the sheriff's office?" Her voice held the same doubt Zachariah had used. "Nobody knows who Joe Kurgar is, but you just happen to come along and figure it out. And the one you happen to figure it out about is the Reverend."

"He's not Joe Krugar, and he's not on that poster."

"And why would that be?"

"I don't know, Hattie. I don't have all the answers. But I saw his face on an old poster. I suspect he's hiding out."

"You *suspect*?" She snorted. "If I had a mind to, I'd chew both your ears off telling you about all the things that *I* suspect—and not one of them has to do with the Reverend. Now, you said your piece, Nate. Go back to that fine life of yours back East."

She started to close the door, but he held it open. Her gaze hardened into a *how-dare-you-out-step-your-bounds* glare. "Get your hand off my door." Burrs roughened the satin of her voice.

The memory of the Krugar Gang almost killing a man in cold blood kept Nate from allowing her to shut him out without her, in turn, making him a promise.

"Promise me you'll stay away from him, Hattie."

Her voice became thorny. "You know what I suspect most of all, Nate? I suspect you're not getting what you want, so you want to make sure I don't get what I want, either."

"What I want is your happiness."

"I'll bet."

"I wouldn't lie to you, Hattie."

"You wouldn't, now?"

"No. I wouldn't."

Thorns disappeared from her voice. "Then tell me where you've been, Nate."

Yearning wrapped around his heart like silk ribbons. There was the look he'd once known in her eyes. It was the same tenderness she'd had when she stood in this same doorway on the night he'd arrived. The moon had cast a beam of light on her as though it was the eye of something divine he'd been following through the darkness. And like that night, he had one last step of his journey—and that was the step through her door and into her arms. She couldn't begin to imagine how far he'd come. But he couldn't tell her, either. Nor could he lie to her, so he let go of the door.

Her eyes glistened at his silence. "At least I *know* where the Reverend's been these past seven years— and it hasn't been in the arms of another woman." She slammed the door. "I've listened long enough to you. Now go away, Nate." Was she weeping? "Go away like you promised."

The door went hazy behind the mist gathering in his eyes as he listened to her muffled sobs. Again, the last step of his journey was one he couldn't take, and by falling short, all he'd done was hurt the person he loved the most. "I'm sorry, Hattie," he whispered. "I'm sorry I can't tell you where I've been."

Because the fact was, his starting point had been more of an abyss than a place.

~*~

As the fading thuds of horse hooves indicated Nate had fulfilled his promise, Hattie sagged against the door. If only she could lock out the hailstorm of hurt that kept finding its way in and pelting her. *I don't want you to go, Nate. I want to see you every day for the rest of my life.* But if she couldn't trust him to be faithful to her, he'd only hurt her more.

Would her pa soon find her and come knocking on her door as well?

Tears spilled onto her cheeks as she closed her eyes. "Why can't they just go away and leave me alone, Lord?"

Two old scars, one cut into the heart of the woman; one cut deeper into the heart of the girl. Each of Nate's good-byes cut his wound deeper. Each day her father stayed in town cut that one deeper. He was so close, she could almost feel him—or more so, the absence of him in her early years.

~*~

"Hattie ain't got no pa." A ring of children caged her in on the school grounds. "And she's always itching 'cause she's got fleas." A rock hit her in the head and struck her down. She landed in the mud.

Trying not to cry, she clutched a handful of prickly burlap, now soiled. When she got home, her ma would be mad because she'd have to scrub it clean. No one else in school had to wear an itchy burlap dress. Maybe, if she had a pa, she wouldn't have to wear one either. She wanted a pa real bad. But maybe she didn't have one because he didn't want her.

~*~

Hattie sank to the floor. "How does a life get so muddled up, Lord? When a man comes back for a woman after he's betrayed her trust...? When a father comes looking for a daughter after she's all grown up...?" Hattie let her sobs go.

"My ma said that my pa didn't know she was with child," she said to God. "But how could he not figure that out? He'd united with a woman, the woman ran away, and he just plain let her go. If that doesn't add up to 'the woman's carrying your baby,' then the man's so dimwitted he can't count to three." She let out a listless chuckle that didn't relieve the pain. "So what made him figure it out now all of a sudden?

"And the way Nate forced the door open." She dabbed at her eyes. "He's never done anything like that before. He was trying to make me listen, but listen to what? Everything he's said about the Reverend, that's just nonsense—isn't it, Lord?"

She'd agreed with Nate that there was something not right about the Reverend, but accusing him of being in an old poster of the Krugar Gang was too far-fetched.

She sat on the floor, elbows on knees, hands clasped below her chin. "I don't want to be alone anymore, Lord. But come to think of it, I never knew a man who'd left me anything other than alone. Until Zachariah came along. I saw in the brotherly way he cared about me what You were all about, Jesus. So that's why I want to marry a man who believes in You. And that naturally leads me to the Reverend—doesn't it?

"But what will he think about my past, being a preacher and all? I still haven't told him I'd worked in the saloon. Zachariah said that You'd provide the right time to tell him, but it's been seven years, Lord, so a person might think You'd have provided the right time by now. So what am I doing wrong, Lord?" Something deep inside her whimpered the truth. *I never told the Reverend because I don't want to marry him.*

Nate was the one she'd always wanted to marry, the one she'd always hurt for. He was the salve. But he was also the knife.

And as for a father, she'd always yearned for a pa to make her ma's work easier and to chase away the things that frightened her at night—but that was when she was a child. She didn't need a pa now—and she especially didn't want one who'd hurt her by not being there when she *did* need one.

Happiness. That's what she'd always wanted. But for some reason, that's what kept steering clear of her. She fell to her knees and buried her face in her hands. *Help me Sweet Jesus.*

18

"There are a lot of memories here."

"Yes, Mother, there are."

A week passed since Nate had promised to leave Hattie alone forever, and he'd stayed true to his word. Nate's business in Ramsden was nearly completed, and he was left only with an ache in his chest and a hope his warning about the Reverend would sink into Hattie's brain. Even ensuring Tilly came through with the money wasn't necessary, because Nate had wired money from his bank and bought the house Doctor Hinkle had told him about.

Sympathizing with Nate's mother's plight, Nate's employer assured him his job would be waiting, but warned him to be back soon. Nate told his employer he'd leave within the week, after he moved his mother's belongings into her new home. Moving wouldn't be an easy task, not because of the items themselves, but because of who they'd once belonged to.

"These are the bookends I gave Marcus for Christmas." His mother picked up a carving of a horse's head and hugged it to her fragile body. "I had them made especially for him. And this is the pen and inkwell I gave him for our anniversary." Each item in Marcus's office stirred a faraway smile from her, but for Nate they were nothing but remnants of a past he'd have to force himself to face, piece by painful piece. And there were so many pieces.

Each book, each pen, each piece of paper he touched scorched him with a memory of the family business and how poorly he'd fitted into it. He picked up one of the old business records. Humming a jaunty tune, he hid from his mother that his hands trembled on the cool leather binding poisoned by Marcus's hand.

~*~

"What do you reckon we should do now, son?"

Nate was fourteen years old and on his first time out driving their cattle. Marcus had appointed him trail boss. Due to his excellent performance in school, Nate thought it only natural he should start at the top. But Marcus had no use for book learning, and a different motive for giving Nate the top position.

"We need to push them two more miles today to keep on schedule," Nate said with confidence. He was well prepared, having based his decision on calculations he'd done before they'd left. He'd studied the map. He'd done the math. This was going to be the most efficient drive Marcus had ever been on.

"So that's your answer?" Marcus said. "Push them another two miles?"

So many miles to go divided by so many days to do it in led to that answer. "Yes, Pa." Nate slid the notes he kept back into his saddlebag.

Marcus rode up to him, retrieved the calculations, and tossed the book to the trampled ground. "If you opened your eyes instead of a book, you'd see these longhorns already had a hard day. You can't push them anymore because they're dead tired. Not only that, but two more miles in this hard terrain will bring us past nightfall, and we won't be able to see a thing. We could drive them right off a cliff, for Pete's sake. Now you go tell Zachariah we're putting up camp for the night. He'll know what to do." And he mumbled, "Glad someone around here has some sense."

~*~

The ledger fell from Nate's hand.

"Is everything all right?" his mother asked.

No, it wasn't. Nate wanted to escape from the house and leave this daunting task solely to her. She could heap all the memorabilia into a pile and light a match to it all. Let the memories of Marcus and the business go up in flames.

The sight of his delicate mother, however, pulled him together. He wrapped his pain into a neat, little package of professional practicality. "Everything in here had to do with the cattle business. The books, the desk, his chair—they're no longer needed."

She glanced around at the room where Marcus had spent most of his time. "*I* need them."

"You're going from a fourteen-room ranch to a four-room house." Though small, the house was practical, so long as she could be sensible. "Not everything will fit, Mother. You need to discern what's important and what—"

"Everything in this room is important to me. I'll find room for it." Innocent of the torment she was putting him through, she began to weep. He pulled her into his arms.

Stoic, he glanced over her head at the massive desk and tufted chair where Marcus used to sit and blatantly scribble out the numbers Nate had entered into the books. Marcus gave him the figures, but wrote illegibly and would grumble if asked for clarification, so Nate would have to guess at the numbers. One way or another, Marcus would rig things so he'd find fault with Nate. He wanted a cowhand for a son, not an accountant.

"I know he was hard on you," his mother said. "After you'd left to go back to college, he was sorry for the way he treated you. It broke his heart. He loved you, and had only the best in mind for you."

So, that's what Marcus had told her—that he'd sent Nate off to college. "The best in mind" was an interesting twist in phrase. No, Nate wouldn't tell her where Marcus had *really* sent him, because it would break her heart.

Instead, staring at the empty chair, he bit back his bitterness. She had always been caught between a man consumed with goals and comforting a son who couldn't meet them. She loved them both, and because Nate loved her, he couldn't deny the gentle woman in his arms her sentiments. "Why don't you go through the rest of the house and take inventory of what you want to keep and what you could sell?"

After she left, Nate forced himself to move the memories into crates and stack the crates against the wall. All the while he hummed to himself to keep remembrances from toppling over on him.

"Nate," his mother called from another room. "Will you help me with this?"

He walked into the dining room, but the sight of what his mother needed help with held him fast. He couldn't move.

"I can't leave this behind," she said. "Not this."

He couldn't even speak, until...*I can't let it fall.* Not this most sacred item.

He rushed over and carefully took from her hands a painting she was trying to take down from over the mantel. "I've got it, Mother." He forced out, "Why don't you go to the bedroom and start packing your own things?"

After she left, he looked into the face of a pretty girl with tumbling golden hair and a mischievous smile. Holding the portrait, he stumbled to a chair. He couldn't tear his gaze from her, and he got lost in her smiling blue eyes.

Sally.

~*~

Steam rose from the bucket and the water scorched her hands as Hattie dipped her rag. The unforgiving wood bruised her knees as she scoured away the flour that had settled into the knots and cracks of her kitchen floorboards.

It had been a week since Nate had visited her. In town, her ears would perk every time she heard Nate's name, and so she'd learned he was helping his mother move into a new home and would leave soon after, just as he'd promised. She'd never again gaze into his serious eyes; she'd never again touch the softness of his yellow curls between her fingers. Never again would her heart leap at the sound of "Hattie" in his voice. *Never again.* The words made her wither inside.

Though she'd prayed often, and though she knew the Lord was listening, He offered no solution to the ache in her heart. All she could do was continue to pray. And scrub. That's what her mother had always done, wasn't it? Scrubbed away the dirt—and the hurt. She rubbed the floor with the same fury she felt in her heart. Just as she dipped her rag again, there was a rap at the door.

She straightened. *No, it can't be him, because this time he'd promised to stay away.* Nate had never broken a promise. And he'd never promised to be true to her.

She walked toward the window to check before answering. Was it her pa? She had a mind to throw the bucketful of water at him. The Reverend? She wasn't in the mood to talk to him. But the visitor was Zachariah.

Which was odd, because he usually came by with Clayton or Lillian so people wouldn't talk, even though there was nothing between them to talk about. She opened the door. "Is everything all right?"

He took off his hat and held it in front of him. He was always courteous, but she'd never met anyone as refined as Nate. "Just checking to see how you're doing, Hattie. I know there's a lot on your mind." By the way he frowned, he had a lot on his mind, too. "Any thoughts about meeting your pa?"

She walked back into the kitchen, squeezed out the rag, and started scrubbing the floor again. "Not a one."

"He asked about you again today."

She scrubbed at the flour as though it were pitch. "He should have asked about me twenty-five years ago."

"Maybe he didn't suspect…"

"So what made him suspect he's got a daughter now? What put the hornet in his hat to come looking for me now that I'm…?" The soreness of bone on wood wasn't enough to keep the crack out of her voice. "Now that I don't need him anymore?"

"I lost my pa when I was a boy, too. But I can't

imagine how hard it was for you going through what you went through. You got a right to be sore at him, and I can't tell you what to do, but if you need an ear to listen, I've got two I can lend you." He hesitated, which meant he was getting ready to say what he'd really come for. "Has Nate been around?"

Hattie dipped the rag, wrung it out, and slopped it back on the floor. Her hands burned. The water hadn't gotten any cooler, and this conversation wasn't getting any better. "I haven't seen him since last week."

"Last week?" His voice rose with an edge of irritation. "You should have told me about that visit, Hattie. I'll put him in jail so he won't bother you no more."

"No. He needs to help his mother move. Besides," she said with effort, "he promised he won't be back."

Zachariah's worry furrowed deep wrinkles into his brow. "Did he say anything about the Reverend?"

"Just something silly."

"Silly like what?"

She looked up at him. "Why are you making such a fuss over such a small thing?"

"Because I need to know. What exactly did Nate say about the Reverend?" He had a *something-else-going-on* look about him.

"Nate just has some strange notion that the Reverend's a crack-shot outlaw." She snorted a listless laugh. "I had all I could do to keep from laughing." And all she could do now not to cry.

Zachariah set determined hands on his hips. "I don't want Nate around you."

"You're more worried about all this nonsense than I am. I'll be fine." As much as she liked Zachariah, she wished he'd go away. She scrubbed the floor with exaggerated vigor, trying to get across the point she was too busy for his visit, but he still wasn't budging. This conversation was over—wasn't it?

"There's something I need to tell you about Nate," he said at last.

"Every time I listen to something someone wants to tell me, I find myself not wanting to hear what they're saying."

"You need to hear this." Zachariah fell quiet for a few seconds. "I know where Nate's been these past years."

~*~

Nate sat in a winged chair by an unlit fireplace, unable to look away from the portrait of his beautiful little sister. He'd buried her over a decade ago, but her loss was still a fresh gash in his heart as though she'd died yesterday. Would his wounds ever heal even a little, as his mother's had?

Sally's eyes lured him into the portrait, pulled him deeper into the past to a brisk winter morning that had happened over a decade ago. It was the last day he'd seen her alive.

~*~

"I'm going to marry that boy." Sally's pigtails bounced and her coat swirled around her as she danced around Nate. She was sixteen and silly over Zachariah.

Nate loathed the sight of him. Nate limped as he walked. The day before, he'd tried once again to earn his father's respect, and after several kicks and falls he'd finally succeeded at roping a cow. But when he looked over to see if

Marcus was watching, Marcus was too busy praising Zachariah for breaking in a horse.

"Hurry up, you slow poke." Sally tugged at Nate's hand. "If you don't get there in time, you'll get the switch."

It was Nate's turn that day to fire up the stove before school started. But every bone in his body felt broken, and he was in no mood for rushing. He yanked his hand away from hers. "Go on without me."

"But Nate—"

"Just leave me alone."

She hesitated and then ran on ahead, until she was out of sight. Eventually, Nate met up with Zachariah and Hattie.

"Where's Sally?" Hattie asked, and then smoke in the distance caught her eye.

"You didn't let her go and start the fire, did you?" Zachariah asked Nate.

The next instant, Nate and Zachariah were running to the schoolhouse. Sure enough, they found fire flashing in the windows—and heard Sally screaming from within.

The rest was a blur of pain and panic as he tried to fight his way to her. It was Zachariah who'd finally carried her out. But by then, it was too late.

Zachariah laid her in Nate's arms, and he looked down into a hideously charred and blistered face.

~*~

The portrait trembled in his hands as Nate began to sob. "I'm sorry, Sally. I'm sorry."

~*~

Hattie sat back on her heels, her limbs frozen as

she stared at Zachariah. "You know where Nate's been? And you haven't told me?"

"Marcus told me in confidence before he died," Zachariah said. "He didn't want word getting around."

"What word?" Did Nate have a child somewhere? That thawed her limbs and heated her face. She rubbed the same spot she'd been cleaning over and over again. Her mother had been right. Scrubbing took away some of the sting. But nothing could prepare her for the shock of what Zachariah said next.

"Nate's been in an asylum."

19

An asylum? The news hit Hattie like a lightning bolt behind her eyes, blinding, deafening, and numbing her. She could no longer feel the soaked rag scalding her hands, the pang of her father wanting to make amends too late, and worst of all, the ever-reopening stab of Nate's—unfaithfulness? The flash flared from her head to her feet and illuminated her whole being about Nate's unexplained absence. She could see, hear, smell, taste, and feel only two words. *An asylum?*

"Hattie, are you all right?"

She must have looked pale.

"Let me fetch you a glass of water."

"No, I'm fine." The news of Nate's whereabouts began to shed light on the shadowed corners of common sense. She wanted to be left alone to understand it all. "You need to get back to the office in case someone needs you."

"'Someone' includes you too, Hattie."

"I'll be fine." To prove it to him, she willed her hand to move in circular motions upon the floor to emulate scrubbing. "You should go now."

He hesitated. "You know where I'll be if you need me." The sound of the latch followed his footsteps.

She dropped the rag into the bucket and stared past the watery swirls of flour on the floor.

Remembrances of when she'd worked in the

saloon reawakened, memories of the many times she'd spent sitting by Nate's bedside trying to comfort him. Nights when sobs would splinter his voice as he stared with moist eyes past the ceiling and said over and over, "I'm sorry, Sally. I'm sorry." Tears would roll down his face, droplets she'd dab at, but his soul would only reabsorb—because he couldn't face the truth.

As a young man, he'd continued to revisit that day and to weep as inconsolably as the seventeen-year-old boy who'd held the body of his younger sister. Even now, Hattie turned her head away from the memory of Sally's burnt body. But Nate rocked her lovingly as he sank to the snowy ground, hugging her and weeping. He'd always said it was his job to protect her, and he'd been so tender toward her, guarding her from so much as the prick of a thorn.

Nate loved so deeply.

His love for his sister was the reason he couldn't accept the truth. From the day of her death forward, his mind had twisted things around so that he'd believed her death was Zachariah's fault. It wasn't right, but Nate couldn't help it, and he claimed it was Zachariah's turn to start the fire and blamed him for lollygagging and letting Sally start the fire for him. Because dear Nate couldn't face the fact that she'd died protecting *him* from being punished.

To relive that terrible day over and over again because he couldn't face what had really happened…

Had Nate learned the truth?

He must have. Hattie put her hand to her heart. "Poor Nate. All that time he's been in an asylum healing his mind, and all along I've been accusing him of being with another woman. How could I be so mean to him, Lord?" Nate would be too ashamed to admit to something like that. "But in spite of my accusations, he didn't say a word because—" Her heart leaped. "— because he wouldn't lie to me."

The shock of learning where he'd been receded from Hattie's mind and blazed in her heart.

"Go to him."

She tore off her apron and put on her best dress. She brushed her hair down and along her shoulder, just the way Nate once liked it. Then she headed toward the Powell ranch to close the aching gap between her and him.

~*~

Nate sat in the dining room, weeping, oblivious to his mother working upstairs, unable to put down the portrait.

Sally. Candid, fearless Sally. One moment she was a carefree girl expressing her joy by skipping, the next moment a headstrong woman expressing her opinions by debating, but always Sally. She'd poured piano music and singing from the music room. With her insistence that girls should be allowed to go on cattle drives, she'd stirred debate at a dinner table occupied by a father otherwise absorbed with his business, a brother engaged in books, and a mother concerned with proper etiquette. Sally was the passion that had once filled a home. Without her the house was too big, too quiet, and too empty.

The portrait portrayed a hint of the saucy smile that had brightened her face and everyone's heart. Though Aunt Sarah had commissioned the painting to be a "serious and sensible likeness of a proper young lady," apparently the artist knew he couldn't capture who Sally really was without her up-to-something smile. In the end, Sally had defied even prudish Aunt Sarah, and Nate smiled at her through his tears for doing that.

Sally couldn't be harnessed. She was a parents' challenge to raise and an older brother's charge to protect. He stared into her blue eyes. Not only had he failed in his task to protect her, but he'd been the very catalyst that drove her to her death.

He leaned his forehead against the image, wishing to hold her. So many times, he'd pleaded with God to send him back in time and to take his life instead of hers. The never-ending grief of losing Sally had been worse than death. Time never dulled the pain but only created paths upon paths of an ever-enlarging labyrinth of wishing and regretting, which all originated at one unforgiving moment. A moment that had once held him prisoner. A moment in which its walls grew tall as time and its corridors endless as eternity.

For years, he'd try to escape only to find that once again he'd made one big circle that brought him back to the beginning. There he'd find Sally's body limp in his arms once again, with her skin black and blistered, the stench of her charred hair sickening. There were also the sobs of a young man begging her for forgiveness because he couldn't forgive himself, and that was the darkness, the never-ending night. He hated himself. Loathed himself. Wished time and time again that the charred body he couldn't get away from was his own.

In the past, it was Hattie who'd always brought him out. Her whispers would lead him back to the light. And the light was the way she'd smiled at him, stroked his hair, and the moist touch of her soft lips upon his forehead. He'd always taken for granted she'd be there to lead him out of his melancholy, until one day, she wasn't.

He vaguely remembered sitting in tubs of extreme water temperatures, drinking a horrible-tasting solution and vomiting, and being dragged into an enclosure someone had called "The Cottage for the Hopeless."

During the years he'd spent in the cottage, he imagined he'd gone from sitting in a corner of his room rocking and apologizing to the ghost of his sister to lying in bed, staring vacantly at the ceiling, and drooling the same words. "I'm sorry, Sally. I'm sorry."

Hattie's voice and the touch of her hand had always guided him back from his melancholy. But now there was no voice to follow, and without Hattie, Nate was left a babbling lunatic. *Where are you, Hattie? I need you.*

He knew the answer then, and he knew the answer now. Hattie was gone and rightfully so. He'd shunned her love by getting engaged to Lillian, a woman he had no feelings for. He'd traded love for hate. Forfeited Hattie's loyalty for a chance to lash out at Zachariah, Marcus's pride and joy. But now Nate knew what was important, because without Hattie, there was no longer a light to come back to.

Or a reason to come back at all.

~*~

No one answered Hattie's knock at the Powell ranch, so she let herself in. Never being in this house before, she hesitated in the foyer. Never had she seen a room so big and so empty but for an ornamental vase on a pedestal.

Where was he? Should she go up the stairs or down the hallway? A familiar sob directed her down the hall and to a room where she found Nate lost in a picture of his sister, and weeping.

Hattie leaned her head against the doorframe, unable to fathom his torment. She ached at the sight of his blond hair disheveled, his fine posture slumped, and his blue eyes shining with tears.

"Hattie," he sobbed, "where are you?"

She cocked her head. This was the same state of melancholy she'd seen him in many times before. But never had he spoken her name. Her footsteps whispered as she walked into the room, but he seemed far away and didn't look up. She lifted the portrait out of his hands and, setting it aside, knelt in front of him. She touched his chin and then tilted his eyes to meet hers.

At first, his gaze fastened upon her with uncertainty, then with wonder. His blue eyes filled with tenderness. "Hattie?"

"Yes, Nate."

"I let her die. I let my beautiful little sister die."

In the past, not only had she comforted him in the loss of his sister, but she'd kept him from getting up and killing Zachariah whom he'd blamed. And at this moment, she realized that Nate had been gone longer than seven years. He'd been gone since the day his sister had died. Now, he was back because someone in the asylum, by the grace of God, had helped him face the truth. She wanted to kiss that doctor.

She wiped a teardrop from his eye. Feeling the moisture on her skin, she realized his soul wouldn't reabsorb this tear, because something about him was new. "I'm here, Nate," she whispered. Her mouth touched his, and his lips closed upon hers, accepting her tender kiss.

Their lips parted, but their gazes didn't. His fingertips trembled across her temple and swept into her hair. He looked away to watch his hand stroke the length along her shoulder. Then he looked back into her eyes as though he were truly seeing her for the first time. "Hattie," he said with certainty.

And then he kissed her deeply.

20

When Nate woke up the next morning, he could still taste the sweetness of Hattie's lips. He'd dreamt about her all night and then rose with the dawn, eager to finish the packing that needed to be done today so he could see her again. He started filling the wagon with his mother's belongings while he whistled.

Even the boxes filled with Marcus's business books had lost their sting.

Nate's mother appeared at the top of the stairs carrying a dress box. "I'm glad to find you in such good spirits," she said in a flat voice.

His whistling stopped at the sight of her.

The black dress on her slight frame made her look more like a shadow than a person.

He hoped her new home would bring her out of the gloom of Marcus's death, but in the meantime, he'd try to brighten her mood with his charm. Nate ran up the stairs and took the box from her. "I shall scold you, Mother, if I see you carrying one more thing. Your duty is to drink tea and to tell *me* what you want moved."

"'In good spirits' is far too inadequate a phrase to describe you today." Her dullness sought to draw him under the same cloud.

"It's a beautiful day. Why should I not be in good—"

"I saw her from the window."

He froze, his euphoria punctured. So that was the reason behind her frown.

The two women he loved had always turned their gazes away from one another, one with pride, and the other with shame.

"She's the reason you came back, isn't she?"

Nate couldn't deny it. "Yes, Mother, she is." He tried to end the discussion by escaping toward the door. "I'll put this box in the wagon where it won't get crushed—"

"No." She looked down at her colorless clothes as though she'd never wear anything else. Then she looked at the dress box Nate was carrying. "Give it to her."

He stopped short. Had he heard correctly?

"I've never worn it and never shall."

Had she resigned to forever remain nothing more than Marcus's widow? Nate wouldn't press her, not now. Instead, he opened the box.

"It would look lovely on...Hattie," she said.

Did she know about the dress he'd bought Hattie long ago? Regardless, the gesture conveyed her utmost effort to accept that he loved Hattie and always would.

He succumbed to her peace offering. "Yes, Mother, it would look lovely on her." He kissed her on the cheek.

~*~

Hattie danced while she baked her pies, sang as she drove her wagon to Kate's Eatery, and hummed as Clayton and Zachariah came over to help. But while Clayton brought in some pies, Zachariah lagged behind.

"I see you're in good spirits today," Zachariah said.

"Why shouldn't I be?" she said. "The sky is blue, and the sun's a-shining."

"The sun's not all that's shining."

Did Zachariah suspect…? *Well, let him.*

She'd never been this happy with the Reverend, and as much as she loved Zachariah as a brother, her relationship with Nate was none of his business. She handed him a couple pies and picked up two more. Carrying them into Kate's, she said over her shoulder at him, "Can't a person be in a good mood without raising questions?"

Anticipating Nate would show up that afternoon, Hattie returned home and cleaned her house, and then cleaned herself up. She put on her best dress, an old-fashioned floral calico.

When he knocked, she rushed to the door but restrained herself from throwing it open. A woman shouldn't look too eager. But the sight of him dressed in a light gray suit that showed off his blue eyes and yellow hair made her heart race. When he handed her a box tied with a fancy ribbon, she scowled and smiled at him at the same time. "I should have known."

"I can't take the credit," he said. "This isn't from me."

Then who could it possibly be from?

He must have read the question on her face. "It's from Mother."

Hattie was sure the question on her face deepened. "She knows about us?"

"She always has, Hattie."

Yes, she always had. Back when Hattie worked in the saloon, Nate's mother would sully the hem of her dress crossing a mucky street before coming within twenty feet of Hattie.

"Well," he said, "are you going to open the box?"

Given the tension between her mother and her, Hattie preferred to keep the cover on and hand it back. Had Nate's mother given her one of those sullied dresses as a reminder of what she thought of her?

"Open it, Hattie."

Nate didn't seem worried, and the box looked pretty tied with that ribbon. She set the box on the table, and carefully unfurled the bow. She would save it if what was inside didn't send her crying to her bed. She slowly lifted the cover. Whatever lay inside was a statement Nate's mother had for her. Was it one of acceptance or insult?

Speechlessness overcame her as she unfolded a red dress embroidered with blue flowers. She rushed to the mirror and held the dress to herself. The colors made her hair shine, her skin glow, and her voice hard to find. "It's...beautiful, Nate. But why?"

In the mirror, she watched a fair-skinned gentleman walk up from behind her darker image until she felt the heat of his breath. "Because she knows I'll never be happy without you," he whispered.

Warmth rushed across her cheeks. Was she blushing?

"Now put it on," Nate said.

"Yes. Yes, of course."

He waited in the kitchen as she threw off the old calico rag and donned the new dress.

White lace lined the neck and her wrists, making every movement of her hands graceful. She waltzed into the dining room and twirled in front of him with the excitement of a princess going to a ball. "How do you like it?"

"No dress will ever be lovely enough to do you justice," he said softly. He opened the door. "But it will do for dinner at Kate's." Outside, a fine buggy drawn by a handsome Morgan waited for her.

As she and Nate rode into town, heads turned and Hattie held back tears of happiness. She was once considered the town's disgrace, but Nate had transformed her into the town belle. Like the finest of gentlemen, he extended his elbow to her and escorted her into Kate's. On his arm, Hattie walked with her chin higher, living a moment she'd always dreamed of. Being by Nate's side.

The eatery was busy, but Kate did a double take. Her eyes grew even wider when they landed on whom Hattie was with. Then she winked an *I-see-a-wedding-coming* to Hattie.

Nate pulled out a chair and seated her as though she were a queen.

Kate waited on them.

"Give the lady anything she wants. If she can't decide, give her everything."

"What would the lady like?" Kate asked as she smiled.

The "lady" chose steak with corn and mashed potatoes.

Never before had she freely walked the streets outside the saloon with one of the town's most prestigious citizens. Never before had she worn a dress so elegant and ladylike.

Women whispered, "Is that Hattie Brown? She looks beautiful."

Men came over and greeted Nate.

It was all dreamlike—the beautiful dress, being

called a lady...but most dreamlike of all was the way Nate gazed at her from across the table. Tenderness filled his blue eyes, and serenity softened his ever-so-serious face as he smiled at her.

Hattie's heart fluttered with the certainty that this was how she wanted to spend every day for the rest of her life.

~*~

Nate couldn't take his eyes off Hattie. Since the day he'd first seen a little girl wearing a burlap dress, this was how he'd longed to see her. Happy. He touched her hand on the table, and the smile on her beautiful face broadened.

She blushed. "Everyone's watching us, Nate."

"You, Hattie. Everyone's watching you because they've never seen anyone so beautiful." The blush in her olive skin deepened, and she looked down in a way he found delightfully girlish. As they ate, his steak had no flavor, and even a tempting slice of apple pie failed to steal his attention away from the feast his eyes were savoring.

Whatever had summoned Hattie to his house the day before, whatever had compelled her to kiss him so tenderly was a mystery. For the moment, he was content to think of it as magical—as fairytale-like as her transformation into the exotic princess.

She looked at her piece of pie. "You keep feeding me like this, and I won't fit into this new dress anymore."

"Then I'll buy you another dress," he said, remembering how thin she'd been as a child. "You've wanted long enough. There will be plenty for you now."

Her long-lashed eyes glistened with delight as she brought a forkful of apple and golden crust toward her maroon lips. With a slow blink of those arresting eyes, she looked back up. But instead of landing on him, her gaze landed on something behind him.

Something that caused the fork to slip from her hand.

~*~

"Hattie," Nate said. "What's the matter?"

She'd never seen him before, but she knew. *It's him. It has to be.*

An older gentleman walked through the door and found a place to sit. He looked around and then suddenly, his gaze latched onto hers.

She stood. "I have to leave."

Nate turned to the man. "Who is he? What does he want with you?"

Without answering, she left the table while Nate lagged behind to pay.

The stranger pushed back his chair and started to rise as she dashed past him and out the door. Her footsteps quickened along the walk as long-ago memories rushed through her mind. *How dare you leave me and my ma to fend for ourselves. How dare you try to come into my life now.* She had to get away from him. She broke into a run and only stopped when someone grabbed her arm from behind.

"Come on." Nate rushed her to the buggy and helped her inside. He turned the horse around and brought it to a full trot while the man, now standing on the walk, watched them ride down the road.

~*~

"I've never seen you act like that around any man," Nate said. "Who is he? What did he do to you?"

She looked aside, not wanting to yield over the words. "He's my pa."

Nate's jaw dropped. "That Southern gentleman is your father?"

"I don't want to talk about it, Nate. I don't want to talk about anything at the moment." She was too angry. *Make him go away, Lord. I don't want to meet him.*

She and Nate rode along quietly. Memories stirred of that day when she was old enough to fend for herself, and her homesick mother returned to Georgia. Hattie hadn't heard from her since, and the ache of her mother leaving still lingered. Where was she? Why hadn't she written?

Nate stopped the buggy on a hill overlooking the former Powell ranch. He looked down at the house with a fondness she'd never seen in him before. Since he'd come back, he'd taken a paint brush to the front doors, fixed the stairs, and mended the front gate, as if something in him wouldn't leave it looking like the wreck it had become in his absence.

Hattie stood beside him and stared out. "You've worked magic on the place, Nate." Any subject to get her mind off her pa would suit her fine. But she snorted at what she'd just said. *Magic?* "I was a fool to believe I could be anything more than what I really am." She looked down at the dress. "Everything fancy about me an hour ago turned back into rags the moment I saw him, because underneath this fine dress, I'm nothing but a child my pa didn't want and my ma was ashamed of."

"Hattie, don't—"

"Stop pretending, Nate." With glistening eyes, she lifted a handful of the elegant embroidered skirt. "This is just an illusion. You can't restore what's never been. Though you've always tried, because you're a man in love, and love makes a man see things that aren't there."

"You're wrong. I love you because of what *is* there. Not only are you beautiful beyond words, but you have every reason to be proud of what you've become, because you've done it on your own—without the help of your father."

"No, Nate. I've become what I am because of my *other* Father. In heaven."

"Then all the more reason to meet the earthly pa, Hattie. You may never have another chance to forgive him."

"After all the taunting I got as a child because he deserted me? How can I face him after all the grief he's caused me?"

"I don't know how. I just know that you have to, because you're a church-going woman now."

Nate? Preaching to her? "What do you know about forgiveness?"

"I don't know much about faith, but I know about the Bible, because we had to read it in school. And I know more than you'd think about you, Hattie. I know that in one form or another, you've always lived by your principles even when it's hurt you to do so. And you'll do it again, because that's always been the best part of you." He placed steady hands on her shoulders. "You've always been the best part of me, Hattie, and if you look deep inside yourself, you'll discover why that is."

After Nate brought her home that evening, after he'd kissed her a long and sweet good-bye, Hattie took off the dress and put on one of her own. The lovely garment lay on her bed, and she saw in the mirror all that was left of her.

A no-good, once-a-saloon-girl, hard-as-nails Hattie Brown. Her eyes glistened. If folks only knew how frail she really was.

Something Nate said returned to her. *"You've always lived by your principles."*

She snorted a laugh. "Yes, but forgiveness was never one of them." She'd never had to forgive anyone before.

Her feelings toward Nate initially had been a righteous anger, because she'd thought he'd cheated with another woman. And she'd never hated her mother, she'd pitied her. Even with everything Boss had done to her, Hattie held no malice toward him, because in a way she understood him. With Boss, it was strictly business. But this Jonathan Garrison Parker, she couldn't even bring herself to meet him.

She sat on her bed. "Why couldn't he have died like Ma said he had, Lord? Even though it left a big hole in my heart, I was better off when I thought he was gone, because when I learned he was alive, I felt like *I* was the big hole—something he just cut out from his life like you carve out the rot on a potato. Maybe that's why I became a saloon girl. Maybe that's all I really am, Lord. Rot." She glanced at her image again. "This morning, I felt like royalty, and now I'm..." She turned her back to the mirror as the warmth of a tear trickled down her face. "How can I forgive him when he treated me like that, Jesus? I hurt so deep."

It felt as if Jesus wrapped His arms around her, comforting her until she was spent. Then it seemed His arms turned her back to the mirror.

This time she saw a woman wearing a calico dress with a hem down to her ankles, a loose fit around her hips, and a high neckline of white eyelet.

"You've always been the best part of me, Hattie," Nate had said, *"and if you look deep inside yourself, you'll discover why that is."*

She stepped closer to the mirror and looked deeply into the eyes of her image to see what he was talking about. What *was* the best part of her? Deep within the soul of the woman looking back, Hattie saw a Christian woman.

A forgiven woman.

"Jesus, *You're* the best part of me."

21

"Where do you want this, Mother?"

"Put it by the window."

Mother's new house, papered with yellow flowers, had lots of charm. However, it had its drawbacks, which Nate had foreseen and Clayton was all too aware of as their gazes met from either end of Marcus's old desk.

"It won't fit there," Nate said.

She threw up her hands. "Then put it anywhere."

Nate shook his head behind her back, and Clayton shrugged. By the time everything was inside, there was barely a trail wide enough to walk through. Nate turned to his mother. "You can't live like this."

She was unwilling to let go of one piece of furniture that had belonged to Marcus, and she began to weep. "My life is so empty without him."

Nate took her in his arms and glared ahead. Were it not for Zachariah, Nate could have stayed and taken care of his mother. In fact, were it not for Zachariah, Mother would still have the ranch because Nate would have taken care of matters before they'd come to this. If hate could sear, he'd burn a hole through that wall and…no, he couldn't lose control. Not now, not ever. He'd be leaving Zachariah behind in due time. Just a day or two longer in Ramsden, and Hattie would be by his side on a train headed toward a wedding back East. He would ask her properly, of course, but he'd already seen "yes" in the way she'd kissed him.

He'd asked Mother to reconsider moving back East with Hattie and him.

"No," she whimpered. "I won't move away from Marcus's grave. I won't leave him. I don't know why you can't stay here." Her eyes were wide, unaware in her pallid face why Nate couldn't stay.

Marcus had never told his own wife where he'd sent her only living child. Or why. Marcus had never told her about the asylum.

Her life had been disrupted enough. It was best she knew nothing about his rage toward Zachariah, a fury ever boiling beneath the surface.

He'd be gone soon enough, but Mother still needed to be cared for. He looked at the silver-tipped Clayton, a mild-mannered, well-established man to whom a son could entrust his mother. But although this bachelor was past his prime, he was still ten years too young for Mother.

As though he suspected what Nate was thinking, Clayton cleared his throat. "I'll leave you two to work out the details. I mean…where to put things." He left.

"Well. I've got to start putting things in their proper place." Tears dried, Mother started placing the pots and dishes on the kitchen shelves. Meanwhile, Nate looked around him at the clutter he'd be sleeping in tonight—and she'd be living in forever.

He squeezed between a dining table covered with boxes, a settee occupied by a bookcase, and after moving a Chinese vase from it, settled in a winged chair. He shook his head at the mess. If only Mother weren't so stubborn about keeping everything, she could have herself a lovely home.

A lovely home.

On the other extreme, there was Hattie living in that old shack with barely a bed, a stove, and a cooking bench. Hattie who'd known so little all her life. But soon there'd be plenty for her, beyond her dreams.

Unlike backwards Ramsden, Boston was alive with crowds bustling on the sidewalks, horsecars waiting at the ready, and newspaper boys shouting the day's headlines. Even the nights were alive with streetlamps that illuminated the brick facades of three-story houses, one of which belonged to Nate.

Two gnarled maples shaded the stairs of his house during the summer and shed crimson leaves on the walkway during fall. A chandelier hanging in the foyer immediately impressed his guests. There were floor cloths from France, a fireplace with a marble mantel, and his bed was made of ornately-carved walnut. The house boasted twelve large rooms. And each one echoed his loneliness.

Although he'd always carefully chosen his clothes and ached at the rags Hattie wore, dressing a house was a different matter. The house needed her to select the furniture, pillows, and curtains that would fill the rooms with things she liked. The house needed her to transform it into a home, and he wanted to see something of her in every thread.

He leaned back in the chair, imagining himself on the landing of his house with Hattie, his bride. He'd thrust open the door and say to her, "This is where you'll live now, my exotic princess. Make it your castle." Then he'd carry her over the threshold. Warmly content with the awe he imagined on her face, he crossed his ankle over his knee.

But first things first. He'd formally ask her to marry him, plan a special event.

Event? Hearing Hattie say yes to his proposal would be more like a holiday.

But meanwhile…

"Nate, will you help me with this?"

Rushing through the clutter and into the kitchen, he found his mother trying to lift the cast iron frying pan their cook had used back when they were a family of four. Nate heaved it onto the shelf.

Another bulky impracticality.

Mother sighed. "So much work to do, and with church tomorrow…"

Church? Yes, Hattie was now a church-going woman and would require the same of him. He didn't mind going to please her—but there was someone else who wouldn't be so thrilled.

Cadwell. He *was* courting her; Nate had seen them together.

That Hattie had lost interest in Cadwell didn't mean he'd lost interest in her. She was a woman a man wouldn't give up easily. So what would Cadwell do if he saw them together?

He'd already threatened Nate once.

~*~

Sunday morning, a breeze ruffled Hattie's skirt and shawl as she stood by Nellie in the churchyard

Nate rode up with his mother and helped Mrs. Powell down from the wagon. The woman was so refined in everything she did, from the way she offered her hand to Nate to the way she greeted her lady friends with a kiss on the cheek. Nate tended to their horse and then offered to help Hattie with Nellie, but Hattie did it herself. Nate lowered his helping hand.

"Is something wrong?"

She cast a glance at his mother talking—rather, chatting—with Prudence, a doctor's wife and a lady as fine as Mrs. Powell. Wasn't that what a real lady did? Hattie had become accustomed to taking up a hammer and fixing things herself, from nailing down a loose barn board to climbing onto a leaky roof and patching it. Nate," she said, "I don't think I can act like that."

"Like what?"

"Like a helpless damsel."

"You wouldn't be the Hattie Brown I knew if you did."

She hung her head. Her past crept up on her, because the Hattie Brown he'd known was the hardened saloon girl who'd enticed men to drink and then stopped them from shooting up the place when they'd gotten too drunk. Although the Lord had cast her past into the "sea of forgetfulness," now and then it popped up on her.

Nate lifted her chin and gazed at her with eyes as clear as the summer sky. "You should never hang your head."

If that was so, then she'd put him to the test. "Then you won't mind if I sit with you and your mother."

~*~

Nate's heart pounded. He would have been honored to have Hattie sit with him and his mother, but for Cadwell. Nate had even rehearsed an excuse. "The Reverend will be on a pulpit preaching to half the town. That's not the time or place for a man to be jilted."

"Jilted?" Hattie waved a dismissing hand. "I'm not

jilting him. I never loved him, and he cares for me as much as he cares about the weather in Alaska." She looked at Nate with motherly tenderness. "I know you have your...suspicions...about him." She took Nate's hand in both of hers. "But there's nothing to worry about. You know that—right?"

Nate was speechless. Why was she talking to him like a child? Why hadn't she just told him he was acting downright crazy?

"But you're right," she continued. "The Reverend deserves to know that you and I are courting, so I'll talk to him after church to make that clear as day to him."

Nate wanted to say that the Reverend had no problem seeing things "clear as day"—not when he could shoot a hole through the knot in a man's necktie. Nate opened his mouth to offer another excuse, but she cut him short.

"Unless I'll embarrass your mother."

The hurt in her eyes said that any more excuses would offend her. And so he offered her his arm and succumbed to the consequences of whatever Cadwell would dole out—and hoped he and Hattie were long gone before Cadwell could dole it out.

~*~

Poor Nate.

Hattie held Nate's arm as he escorted her toward the church. Her love for him would always include calming his mind. Even though he'd been treated at the asylum, wounds always left scars. "There's no need to worry about the Reverend. He's harmless as a cottontail."

"Mother likes you," he said as they walked. "That's why she gave you the dress."

Hattie touched the skirt. "Giving away your dress is nothing like giving away your son."

His mother joined them. "Hello, Hattie," she said. "I hope you'll be sitting with us."

"Yes, Mrs. Powell." Hattie's heart leaped. "If you don't mind."

"I'd like you to sit by me." In her genteel way, she took Hattie by the elbow and whispered in her ear, "There's something I'd like to talk to you about."

Hattie received some stares as she and Nate walked inside the church. Why did everyone seem to think she belonged to the Reverend? Nate's mother arranged them in the pew so that Hattie sat between son and mother. When Nate looked away, his mother squeezed Hattie's hand.

"Nate's all I've got," his mother whispered. "And I know he's deeply in love with you. Make him stay here, Hattie. Make him stay with you in Ramsden."

The blood left Hattie's face. Yes, Nate had said he had a house and a job in Massachusetts. But he wouldn't expect Hattie to leave Ramsden, would he? She leaned toward his mother, but the opening notes of a hymn, as Lillian started playing the piano, cut their conversation short.

~*~

After singing *Bringing in the Sheaves*, Nate sat down and braced himself for Cadwell's reaction. What would he preach about this time? Murder? Thievery? Those were his areas of expertise, weren't they?

Acting like an oblivious clown, Cadwell stumbled

up to an oak pulpit and tapped his sermon notes into a neater stack. He polished his eyeglasses, put them on, and then polished them again.

Nate fidgeted as everyone else waited patiently for this foolery to run its course.

Then Cadwell perched his hands on the pulpit and looked over his spectacles. A bead of sweat trickled down Nate's collar as Cadwell's gaze locked his for one searing moment. Cadwell cleared his throat and looked down at his notes. "'Thou shalt love thy neighbour as thyself.' Matthew chapter twenty-two verses thirty-five through forty: 'Then one of them, which was a lawyer, asked him a question, tempting him, and saying, "Master, which is the great commandment in the law?" Jesus said unto him, "Thou shalt love the Lord thy God with all thy heart, and with all thy soul, and with all thy mind. This is the first and great commandment. And the second is like unto it, Thou shalt love thy neighbour as thyself. On these two commandments hang all the law and the prophets.'"

Nate tensed. Cadwell wanted to make a point that Nate was sure had nothing to do with brotherly love.

"Please note," Cadwell preached, "that the man who asked Jesus this question was a lawyer and that his intention was to tempt the Lord, not learn something from Him. In scripture, it was always the experts of the law and religion who tried to set a snare for Jesus."

Had Cadwell emphasized "snare"?

"But they never outsmarted our Lord." Cadwell paused. Was he trying to tell Nate that he was too cunning to be outsmarted?

Nate no longer cared about exposing Cadwell. Cadwell was Zachariah's problem. Nate's sole concern now was sweeping Hattie off to Massachusetts before Cadwell knew she was gone.

"First John four, verses twenty to twenty-one has more to say on the subject of loving thy neighbor as thyself." With the exception of that first glare, Cadwell seemed unscathed at the sight of the couple sitting dead center in the third row. "'If a man say, I love God, and hateth his brother, he is a liar: for he that loveth not his brother whom he hath seen, how can he love God whom he hath not seen?'

"Now we know that God created man in His own image, so look around you at the images of God, brethren. This includes the neighbor sitting beside you, in front of you, behind you—"

"What if your neighbor's a woman?" Sometimes Nate's mouth worked faster than his brain, and he regretted speaking.

People sitting around him snapped annoyed gazes at him, including Zachariah, who cast a lingering look.

"Why, that's a good point, Nate." Cadwell grinned. "The scripture applies to women as well as men in this respect. Just because God created you ladies…well…um… you know…"

Someone in the pews offered, "Differently?"

Everyone chuckled. They were not only his audience, but his duped allies.

"Just because God created you ladies—" Cadwell's voice cracked "—differently…well, we all share in the inheritance of Heaven. And so your neighbor includes every man, woman—" he took an unneeded sip of water "—and child sitting here today."

Every person shares in the inheritance of Heaven except you, Cadwell, because if there's a God, He's no lying outlaw. Zachariah's glare nudged Nate to add, *And everyone except me.*

Judging by the nods and "amens," Cadwell knew how to pick his topics.

"First John three, eighteen says, 'My little children, let us not love in word, neither in tongue; but in deed and in truth.' In other words, love is more than just talk. Love is action. Love is extending a helping hand to one another when needs arise. Love is doing everything we can to live together as the body of Christ, and doing so with sincerity." Cadwell read, sipped water, and polished his eyeglasses. "And so brethren—and, um, sisters—I leave you with 1 John 4:11. 'Beloved, if God so loved us, we ought also to love one another.' Can I get an amen?"

Everyone except Nate responded with an enthused, "Amen."

After the ending hymn, Cadwell stood in the doorway to shake hands and bask in compliments for his excellent performance. And what a performance it was. No other way out, Nate followed his mother and Hattie toward him. How long could Cadwell keep up the act?

Mother reached him first. "You preach a good sermon, Reverend." She turned to Nate. "Doesn't he, Nate?"

Nate answered his mother as he eyed Cadwell. "So did Jonah. Am I correct in my recollection that Jonah had ill in mind for them rather than good when he'd preached to the Ninevites?" Nate didn't forget a thing about anything he'd read.

Cadwell's eyes gleamed. "You know your Bible."

Nate glared back. The man was a wolf clothed in sheepskin. "Any heathen can read it."

"Yes, and a heathen should know that 'the word of

God is quick, and powerful, and sharper than any two-edged sword, piercing even to the dividing asunder of soul and spirit, and of the joints and marrow...'"

Was that a threat? "You forgot the rest of the verse...Reverend. Regarding the word of God, it's also '...a discerner of the thoughts and intents of the heart.'"

"We were all heathens once, enemies of God," Cadwell responded.

Nate remained silent, hoping for the chance that there just might be a God so He would personally dole out what Cadwell deserved.

"Sounds like you'd make a better preacher than me, Nate. I hope you'll be joining us again."

In front of the church, Mother chatted with her friends, and Hattie left Nate's side to head toward Cadwell. "I'll tell him about us now, like I promised you I would."

Nate caught her wrist. "Hattie, you don't have to—"

"Everything's fine, Nate. There's nothing to worry about, honey."

He stepped back. Why was she talking to him like a child again?

Hattie slipped away and talked to Cadwell, although Nate couldn't hear a word they were saying.

Cadwell maintained his silliness by dropping his eyeglasses.

Would he lose his temper and charge at Nate here? The answer came sooner than expected when Hattie left Cadwell, but was intercepted by Nate's mother.

And Cadwell headed toward Nate.

Nate took a deep breath.

Cadwell stopped at arm's length and with an

unreadable face, proffered his hand. Others were watching. Nate shook Cadwell's hand and when he did, the Reverend clamped down on his fingers like the jaws of a Gila monster.

Playing the clown, Cadwell tripped so only Nate would hear what he was about to say.

22

"She's a good woman," Cadwell whispered in Nate's ear. "She deserves someone who can marry her—so long as that man treats her with due respect." He walked away leaving Nate speechless.

Hattie was right. Cadwell wasn't in love with her. *But if Cadwell had no intention of ever marrying her, why did he court her?* Nate chuckled to himself. *Because Cadwell knew Hattie wasn't interested in him either, and so he could use her as part of his act without hurting her in a romance much of the town would cheer on.* But why was he acting? And why would an outlaw care about a woman's feelings?

Nate shrugged it off. Cadwell was a man of mystery, but a mystery Nate no longer had to solve—now that Hattie was his. She and his mother looked as if they were already family as they stood arm in arm talking to Clayton. Nate felt a foot taller as he watched them, and his pride for them spread to his face. But his smile was cut short.

"I understand your mother's moved in. Is that true?"

He stiffened at the deep voice he'd hoped never to hear again. What business was this of Zachariah's? Nate wanted no trouble. "Yes, she's all set."

"Then I reckon you have no more business here in Ramsden."

"Tomorrow I'll make arrangements to leave." Nate started to retreat, but Zachariah added one more thing, which stopped Nate in his tracks.

"Stay away from Hattie. If I see you with her again, I will lock you up. Is that understood?"

The conversations around them converged into a solitary hum as Nate's fingers collected into a fist. How dare Zachariah tell him to stay away from Hattie. She would be Mrs. Powell with or without Zachariah's high and mighty approval. Who made him king of this sun-scorched empire? Nate stepped toward Zachariah. "Who do you think—"

Hattie latched onto Nate's elbow. "Who do you think is going to take me home, Zachariah?" She turned to Nate. "Clayton's horse has a loose shoe, so I loaned him Nellie. Your mother and I have been waiting for you by the wagon."

Zachariah eyed Nate but spoke to Hattie. "The Reverend's a good man. You might reconsider—"

"Reconsider what, Zachariah?" Nate glowered.

"Reconsider what's best for her," Zachariah glowered back.

"And by being the sheriff," Nate said, "you just happen to know what that is."

Hattie tightened her grip on his arm as if she were not only holding him back but holding him together.

"I know what *isn't* best for her."

If bullets could have shot out of his eyes, Nate would have filled Zachariah with lead.

"I love you like a brother, Zachariah." Hattie shook her head. "But I have a mind of my own and speaking to the Reverend was my mind, not Nate's."

Zachariah crossed his arms. He didn't like that one bit. There was something else he would like even less.

"She asked me to take her home, Zachariah," Nate said. *So how can you arrest me in front of her for doing that?* Nate savored the sweet defeat as Zachariah clenched his jaw. But by the glare in Zachariah's eyes that defeat was only temporary. Although Cadwell had given up without a battle, Zachariah was apt to put up an entire war.

~*~

The wagon jarred Hattie as she sat in silence, as did Nate.

He'd hardly said a word on the way to his mother's home. As they headed toward Hattie's house, he glared ahead at a sandy road worn into a brown, brittle field.

What was he thinking about? She hoped not about Zachariah. Not with the way Nate's arm quivered beneath her hand. Years ago, Nate's anger toward Zachariah had been one in which Nate would go into a melancholy mood and threaten to kill him, but she'd held him back. Did Nate still have that rage?

Learning he'd been true to her had thrilled her to the core. Furthermore, going to church when he'd once called the Bible a book of fairytales showed a change in Nate. But had he changed enough? Despite the dry heat and a glaring sun, a chill ran through her. *How bad had he gotten to have required treatment at an asylum?*

She stared into the past, to one near-disastrous day when Lillian was trapped in a burning building. It was a day that echoed an even more distant and tragic event when Sally, Nate's sister, had died in a fire. It had been Nate's turn to get the stove going in the schoolhouse that morning, but he was lollygagging so

Sally went ahead and fired it up for him. He couldn't face that she'd died trying to keep him out of trouble, so he'd convinced himself it was Zachariah's turn to get the stove going. Nate had wanted to kill Zachariah ever since.

Then, when the past came back to haunt them and Lillian almost died in a fire, Nate was gone the very next day. Rumor was his father had demanded Nate forget about marriage and finish school. *But...*

She stared at memories of a father trying to console a weeping son and a marriage between Zachariah and Lillian that happened too soon after. *But his father had sent Nate to the asylum instead.* She threw her hand over her mouth. *Because his father knew Nate had set that second fire.* It was hatred that had stolen Nate's senses. How could she have not seen this sooner? "It's best you stay away from Zachariah."

"Funny." Nate's voice was as dry as the scorching sun. "That's the same thing he said about you—except he also threatened to throw me in jail."

Zachariah wasn't a man who spoke warnings lightly.

Much to the protest of a cranky rooster, they pulled up in front of Hattie's house.

Nate sat, reins in his hands, staring at the chickens squabbling behind a wire fence.

She bit her lip on her worry as she put her hand over Nate's still-trembling fingers. "Everything will be all right," she said in her most soothing voice.

He stared ahead. "Yes, everything *will* be all right." He turned to her. "I had a better place in mind to do this, but...Hattie, will you do me the honor of becoming my wife?"

A breeze fondled his hair as she gazed into his

face. Her breath caught in her throat at how handsome he was. But there were hitches in becoming his wife. "Let's not talk about this now, Nate."

He frowned. "I was under the impression you loved me."

"I *do* love you-"

"Then what's there to talk about? We can't put this off, not with Zachariah hankering to lock me up to keep us apart. Hattie, the sooner we leave for Massachusetts, the better."

And that was the biggest hitch. "We need to discuss going to Massachusetts."

"What's there to discuss? I have a fine house and a great job. We have everything there."

"*You* have everything there. I've made a life for myself here." She shook her head at him, because there was something else. "Love's clouded you, Nate, because you forget I'm a half breed and not everybody can accept that like you do. But most of all, I don't want to leave Ramsden. I have friends here who have become family. And now that I'm getting close to your mother—"

"You know I can't stay here." The tremor in his arms deepened. "You've seen the way Zachariah treats me."

She closed her eyes. How could she tell Nate how much Zachariah meant to her? That he was the brother she couldn't leave behind? How could she tell Nate that he was to blame for making Zachariah his enemy by wrongfully blaming Zachariah for Sally's death and trying to retaliate by using Lillian, whom Zachariah loved? It was a good thing Zachariah was a godly man, because otherwise Nate would have fared much worse. Zachariah had good reason to hate Nate. Yet at one time, they'd been the best of friends.

"What happened to the two of you?"

His eyes gleamed. "You know what happened."

She knew a lot more than he realized. Dare she say it? "Didn't they help you?"

"They?" His voice flattened. "Who are you talking about?"

There was no use keeping it from him. "I know where you've been, Nate. You poor soul."

He hesitated. "And where exactly is that?"

She squeezed his hand. "An asylum." She hoped uncovering the secret between them would draw them closer together, that he would wrap his arms around her. Instead, his eyes hardened.

"How do you know about that?" He raised his voice. "Who told you where I've been?"

The blood left her face. He'd never looked at her with such fury in his eyes. She refused to answer. Couldn't answer. The fury...

"Get out, Hattie. Get out of the buggy."

She stood stiffly in front of her house, watching Nate's wagon speed down the road in a storm of dust and the fury of his humiliation. He hadn't wanted her to know he'd been in an asylum. She'd embarrassed him. No, she'd done something worse, because Nate was no fool. He would figure out who had told her about the asylum, and when he did...

She regretted loaning her horse to Clayton. Now she was unable to ride out and warn Zachariah. She prayed God would protect him and his family.

23

"Giddy up!"

Though the horse was already running at a fast clip, Nate cracked the reins again. He had to get away from Hattie and her pity. The way he used to behave in front of her, sobbing to the ghost of his sister, had been pathetic. But for Hattie to know he'd been in an asylum was outright humiliating. No wonder she'd talked to him like a child. *"You poor soul."* He didn't want her pity; he wanted her respect. More so, he'd never asked to be sent to a place where the doctors were crazier than the patients.

~*~

Though Nate's mind was trapped in a maze, he had a dreamlike awareness of his surroundings. His room was a gray box that accommodated a bed with a hard mattress and a chair no one ever sat in. He sat in his nightshirt in a corner, rocking. The drapes were drawn and the darkness was cool but for a splinter of sunlight that cast a fingertip of heat on his knee. Tears trickled down his face as he begged his sister's forgiveness yet again.

"I'm sorry, Sally. I'm sorry."

He'd been trapped inside himself for so long. Where was Hattie? It was she who would call his name, her voice that would guide him out.

"Pick him up." This voice belonged to a man and came from a faraway place Nate didn't care about.

Something clamped down on his arms and bruised him

as they tugged him to his feet. Sally's body tumbled from his arms, and he groped for her as he was pulled away.

He squinted from a sudden burst of light. He tried to shield his eyes, but the clamps wouldn't let him. A creak and a click, and the brightness disappeared.

"Do you think this will work on him? Everything else we've tried hasn't."

A stranger's face appeared in front of Nate's in the fog. The man had eyeglasses. Studious men wore eyeglasses. But Nate had seen this man in the fog before, and he had no name for him, only a feeling. Pain.

"Give him this," Pain said. "It's calomel. It'll purge him of impurities."

A tin cup pressed against Nate's lips. He turned away.

"Drink it."

Pain forced Nate's mouth open, and Nate choked on thick, tasteless fluid. He spat it out, but Pain forced more in so that Nate felt like he was drowning. The fluid burned his throat with each forced gulp.

The hands of Pain released him, and the other men in the fog stepped back and waited.

Waited for what?

Nate's stomach began to sour. Then cramp.

Pain said, "Get the bucket ready."

Nate doubled over with spasms as the contents of his stomach spewed from his mouth. He retched again. He kept vomiting until there were only dry heaves left. Finally, when his stomach had given up everything and his strength had been spent so that he trembled, he collapsed.

"Nate," Pain demanded. "Nate Powell. Answer me."

But the treatment had only served to send Nate deeper into himself to retreat from the nausea. And that enraged Pain.

"What's wrong with you?" Pain shouted. "I've used

spinning boards with you, temperature fluctuations, purgatives, everything I can think of. Nothing works on you. You're obstinate!"

"Should you be talking like this in front of him?"

Pain threw up his hands. "What does it matter? He can't hear a word we're saying." Pain put his spectacled face so close to Nate's, Nate could see the pores on his nose. "And that's because you're too stubborn to come out of your melancholy." Pain waved his hand. "Well, you can stay in there for all I care. I give up. Get him out of my sight."

~*~

They'd moved Nate to "The Cottage for the Hopeless," which was little more than a warehouse to keep the unwanted. But while his soul remained trapped in a deep, dark pit, at last this was a place where they left his body alone. So it wasn't the doctors who'd "cured his mind" as Hattie had thought. He would have been there forever, but for a most unusual woman.

He was sobbing to Sally as he'd been doing for an eternity, when he heard a faraway voice. This time it belonged to a woman.

"I'm here for you, Nathan, you dear child of God."

Was it Hattie's voice? It didn't sound like her, and those were strange words for her to say. But she touched his hand so differently from the grabbing he'd become accustomed to. It was a touch so gentle, a groan filled his soul and a tear trickled down his temple.

Hattie.

It had been so long since he'd seen her. He yearned to see her beautiful smile again. She was and had always been the only reason he went back to a world that had caused him so much grief.

But he felt as if he'd been asleep a hundred years. Rousing himself from the slumber was like swimming from the depths of the ocean up to the surface. Opening his eyelids was like lifting anvils. But when he saw her at last, what started as a surge of infuriation from within came out as a mumble. "Who in blazes are you?"

Standing by his bedside was a middle-aged woman wearing a gray dress and a white apron. Streaks of silver glimmered at the temples of her coal-black hair, and her brown face broke into a grin. "If this Sally loved you as much as you loved her, I'd say she never blamed you in the first place."

"You don't know what you're talking about." His voice was that of an old man's. What was wrong with him?

"Oh, I think I understand more than you're giving me credit for," she said with a chuckle. "In fact, I don't think it's this Sally who needs to forgive you at all. I'd say it's you who needs to forgive yourself, you dear child of God."

"Don't call me that. I don't believe in your religious rubbish." He tried to get out of bed to chase her away but couldn't move. His heart pounded with panic.

"Your legs have gone weak from lack of use." She opened the drapes and let in a flood of daylight. "You've been lying in that bed a long time."

"Where am I?" He demanded in a hoarse voice.

"I think you know where you are."

As cloudiness cleared from his head, nightmares of being sick and scalded turned into memories. "I'm in an asylum." His heart thundered. "How long have I been here?"

"Suffice it to say that you've been laid up long enough that you'll have to learn how to walk all over again."

Another failed attempt to move his legs proved her right. "You're not a doctor. Who are you?"

She gave an easy laugh. "A doctor? Do I look like a doctor to you?" She held up a mop. "I'm the cleaning woman, and I'm here to clean your room, Nathan, you dear child of God."

He hated her calling him that. "I want another cleaning woman."

She put a hand over the apron band around her thick waist. "Why? You don't like the job I'm doing?"

"I don't like you."

"Why not? I'm just doing what I'm paid to do. Don't you want a clean room? 'Clean room, sound mind' they seem to think around here." She took a deep breath, and started mopping.

"But you think that cleanliness is next to Godliness," he muttered.

"No," she answered. "I think the only thing next to Godliness is Godliness."

He huffed. "So who are you? Priscilla?"

She stooped to mop under his bed. "To know that name, you have to know a little about the Bible."

"I've read Gulliver's Travels *as well," he said, "but I don't believe in Lilliputians."*

She laughed at his sarcasm as she moved to the other side of his bed. "Yup. Mopping and dusting. That's what I do around here."

"And talk a lot."

"You don't like me talking? Then I'll be quiet." She worked in silence, and that was even more maddening.

"Well," he demanded in a small voice, "say something."

"What do you want me to tell you?"

"I want to know what's wrong with me."

She lifted the mop. "Have you forgotten?"

But he persisted. "How long have you been working here?"

"Long enough to know every scuff on these floors," she said, looking down as if she were familiar with every scratch.

"Then you've been here long enough to know something about lunacy. What do you think is wrong with me?"

"You really want to know what I think?"

"I asked, didn't I?"

She stopped working and leaned on the mop. "From the first day I saw you, you never struck me as a man who was sick in the head so much as you were sick in the heart."

How dare she say that. He demanded with a feeble finger, "Get out of here."

~*~

Nate cracked the reins and cursed the Morgan stallion. "You run like an old nag. Faster!" But it wasn't the horse he wanted to spur so much as it was his thoughts. *How did Hattie find out I was in the asylum?*

To his knowledge, the only ones who knew were Marcus and Aunt Sarah, whom Marcus needed to conduct Nate's business and provide a place where Marcus could tell Nate's mother and everyone else where he'd gone. A proud man like Marcus didn't exactly announce to his community that his son was a lunatic. Marcus wouldn't have told Hattie because as far as he was concerned, she was no more than a place Nate would retreat to when he'd had enough of Marcus's complaints.

So who else might Marcus have told of Nate's whereabouts when he hadn't even told Nate's own mother?

Spinster Aunt Sarah didn't know anyone in

Ramsden, and she was too proud to have spilled a word. She'd likely hidden behind a parasol when she came to the asylum to conduct Nate's business. To his knowledge, she hadn't visited him once, and when he got out, he never visited her either. He'd always disliked her. She was too much like Marcus.

Way too much like Marcus. *"You're as sweet as cinnamon,"* Aunt Sarah would say to Sally and indulge her with dresses, ribbons, and dolls. When Sally turned sixteen, Aunt Sarah commissioned Sally's portrait. But she never gave so much as a stone to Nate, and she'd once said to him with a curled upper lip, *"You know what little boys are made of."*

Nate huffed. *Favorites.*

Suddenly, he knew who Marcus had told about Nate being in the asylum—and who, in turn, had told Hattie.

24

Hattie paced, regretting that she'd told Nate she knew he was in the asylum and worried about Zachariah and his family. A rap on her door stopped her short, and she rushed over to open it hoping Nate had come back. She threw open the door to find an unpleasant surprise.

"Forgive me for my intrusion, but the owner of the saloon told me where to find you," said a stranger whose face flushed pink. With his white hair, fancy white suit, and fair-skin, he looked like a glass of milk, and he appeared to be just as innocent.

Hattie knew her pa was white but never fathomed he'd be this white. She wanted to slam the door in his face. It figured Boss would retaliate for her quitting by telling the last person she wanted to see where she lived.

"I'll be leaving on tomorrow's stagecoach," the stranger said, "and I must talk to you about something of dire importance. May I?" He poked the hat he held in front of him toward the inside of her house.

Arms crossed, she stood in his way. Whatever Jonathan Garrison Parker deemed "of dire importance" was likely important to him alone. Why else would he come looking for her? *Lord, I've got a lot on my mind with Nate. I don't know if I can deal with this man right now. Or ever.*

The Lord's answer began with what she could

do—invite the man inside.

She tossed her hand. "Have a seat."

He accepted the glass of lemonade she offered him but hesitated at the sight of her old dining set with its scratches and worn varnish.

"Not what you're used to, huh?" She smacked the glass on the table with the same bluntness she'd done back when she worked as a saloon girl, because that's how he made her feel. Like an outcast. "Well, do you want to talk or not?"

"I do."

"Then sit down."

He was nothing like what she'd pictured her father would look like. He stood there frozen as she glared at his snow-white suit and shiny silver buttons. Even his shoes were perfect without so much as a scuff. If only her life had been that spotless. It seemed she and her ma had taken all the scuffs and scrapes for him.

"Miss—Henrietta...I—I don't know what to call you by."

Funny, she didn't know what to call him by, either. So she didn't. "Folks around here call me Hattie."

"Then if I may, Miss Hattie." He pulled out her chair and waited on her to sit.

She hesitated. As far as she was concerned, he could wait on her forever, because she'd waited on him almost thirty years. And that was three decades too long. Now, hoping to get things over as quickly as possible, she accommodated him by dropping into the proffered chair.

He sat down slowly and looked deeply at her. "You're a beautiful woman, Miss Hattie. A very beautiful woman. Forgive me, but for some reason, I envisioned a little girl." He cleared his throat and took a sip of lemonade. "If I may say, I didn't anticipate things between us would be this awkward."

"How on earth did you expect things between us to be?" she snapped back.

"I didn't expect you to even be," he said. "That is, until two weeks ago."

How could he not suspect? "My ma ran away while she was still your *slave*, didn't she?" He humbly nodded. "Yes."

"After you and she…?"

His blushed deepened. "I can only imagine that just one hour of our love would produce something as beautiful as you."

"Beautiful?" Hattie's face heated with resentment. "Do you know how ugly it was for me growing up without a father? What it was like to be afraid every night that outlaws would come in and hurt us? What it was like to be six years old with blisters from working so hard and watching my ma work even harder? What it was like to wear rags and go hungry and always feel like I was never going to get warm?" Her eyes burned. "Do you know what it was like to…" She covered her mouth, unwilling or unable to say the rest—*hate myself because my pa didn't give a fig about me?* She tried to swallow her anguish, but it spewed out. "How could you not know about me?"

His eyes glistened. Why did he have to look at her so tenderly? "I beg your forgiveness. Can you pardon a man for being so blind?"

Being a Christian obligated her to forgive him, but he could squirm a bit more for her pardon. "You said something happened two weeks ago. What made you come looking for me now?"

"Your mother's sister paid me a visit."

"You mean my Aunt Henrietta?"

"I do."

Hattie covered her mouth again, this time out of joy. Aunt Henrietta was the only relative Hattie's mother had told her about, though she'd never met her.

Hattie shot to her feet. "Is she in Georgia? Is my mother with her?" Was she going to see her mother again and meet her aunt?

"Henrietta left Georgia soon after the emancipation," he said, "and settled in Iowa where she found work as a cleaning lady in an asylum."

Hattie shrugged off the remote possibility that it could be the same asylum Nate had been in. "Does she know where my mother is?"

"Yes, she does. In a sense."

That was a strange answer. "What kind of sense?"

He hesitated. "She told me that your mother had passed on."

Hattie's dancing heart came to a standstill.

"You have my sincerest condolences." He reached to touch her hand on the table, but she pulled it away.

"I know this is hard on you," he said. "It was hard on me as well when I found out. It still is." He glanced around the room at the faded red drapes and plain wooden walls. A glance from his gleaming eyes indicated "hard" included learning about her. "I understand she'd been sickly for several years." He cleared his throat and took another sip.

"And you come looking for me to tell me that?" Hattie asked flatly.

"Yes. I thought you should know. But I also

wanted to meet you after learning about you from your aunt."

"Why couldn't you just leave it to my aunt to tell me?"

He offered her an injured look. "You think mighty low of me."

Yes, she did, and she tried to drive that point through to him with a hard glare, which he met with soft eyes.

"I truly wish I could establish a better rapport with you," he said. "We are father and daughter."

No they weren't. "You're a stranger."

"No, Miss Hattie, I'm a man you resent because you've never met me. There's a difference." He stared into his glass of foggy lemonade. "I wish I could go back and change it all for you and your dear mother."

Wishing didn't change anything. But there was something Hattie needed to know. "How much did you love her?"

His voice trembled. "Make no mistake; I have loved no woman as much as I loved her. I never married, because I knew I would find happiness with none other than her."

"Then why didn't you marry her?"

"You don't understand. We had to hide our love. This was Georgia."

"You could have come to Ramsden. My mother did. Folks here don't care what color you are."

"If I had left," he said, "I would have forfeited my inheritance."

Is that what had kept them all unhappy? Money?

She walked away from the table and crossed her arms. *Lord, he's not making it easy for me to forgive him.* In fact, she wanted to give him a good tongue lashing but held her temper. "If you've said your piece, I'd like you to leave now."

"I understand." As he came to his feet, he pulled an envelope from his inner pocket and placed it on the table. "I can't change your past, but I can aspire to help your future."

Hattie looked at the thick envelope. "Are you trying to buy my forgiveness?"

"I'm a Christian man, Miss Hattie. My forgiveness has already been purchased." And with that, he left.

25

Nate banged on the door of what might have been a charming two-story house with a white picket fence had it not been for the man who lived there. "Come out, Zachariah." He banged again.

The door flew open, and Zachariah appeared, rifle in hand, a man guarding his family. If there was anyone else in the house, Nate didn't see them nor did he care. His senses had tunneled in on one thing. All he could see, hear, smell, and even taste was the bitterness in front of him in the form of a man with a name he hated so much, he couldn't spit it out a second time.

"What do you want here, Nate?"

Revenge, that's what he wanted. His hands shook, itching for it. His chest tightened, craving it.

"You told Hattie I was in the asylum. You knew because Marcus told you. He didn't even tell his own wife, but he told his hired hand. You took my father from me, you good-for-nothing-"

"I'm warning you." Zachariah raised the rifle. "Get off my property."

But Nate's shoes held fast. "Everyone here thinks you're a sheriff, but behind that badge you're a nothing. And a nothing doesn't tell a Powell what to do."

A small voice came from inside the house. "Why is he yelling at Daddy?"

"Hush, Molly," Lillian said.

Nate barely heard the voices of Zachariah's wife and daughter as he lost his senses and lunged at a man a head taller and forty pounds heavier. The next moment, Nate was on the ground with his arms locked behind his back. He could barely breathe under Zachariah's weight.

"You come to my house, you frighten my family," Zachariah said. "That does it. I've had it with you, Nate."

~*~

Evening had stolen the ray of sunlight that poured from the window and onto the worn table where Hattie had been sitting a long time, chin in hand, looking down at the envelope Jonathan Garrison Parker had left behind. Its thickness, along with his words *"I can't change your past, but I can aspire to help your future,"* were a dead giveaway there was money inside. How much didn't matter, because no amount of money could ever rebuild a person's past.

But then again, his words had been mighty humbling. *"I'm a Christian man, Miss Hattie. My forgiveness has already been purchased."*

"I get the point, Lord," she said.

Another knock at the door, and Hattie perked. Nate had been gone a long time. She peeked out the window, and when she saw that it was Zachariah, she knew where Nate had been. Thank God Zachariah was all right. Was his family all right as well?

"Howdy, Hattie." The flatness in his voice when she opened the door told her that everybody was fine but that Zachariah was steaming mad.

"This isn't a social call, is it?" she said.

"No, it ain't. I'm here on business."

Nate, what did you do? "And what business would that be?" As if she had to ask.

"I've got Nate locked up in the jailhouse, I'm putting him on tomorrow's stagecoach, and I don't want you anywhere near him in the meantime."

The blood left her face. "You can't do that, Zachariah."

"I can, and I did." He raised his voice, which meant he'd reached his wit's end. "He came to my house and scared my family half to death. So, look here, Hattie. I'm the sheriff of this here town, and I aim to protect the people in it, and that includes my family as well as you. You've been letting him court you and encouraging him to stick around. I want him gone."

If only she hadn't told Nate she knew about the asylum. "Are you telling me I can't even visit him in jail?"

"I don't want you within a mile of him. I told you, he's not right in the head."

"That's because he lost his sister," she pleaded.

"I loved Sally, too. But I can't afford the luxury of concerning myself with the why behind Nate's conduct, because I have to concern myself with the fact that he's a dangerous man and that I can't have him around you or this town any longer."

Hattie crossed her arms. Zachariah wasn't going to tell her what to do when her heart said otherwise. "You have no right to run my life, Zachariah. You're not my boss." She looked Heavenward. "He is."

"And He put me in charge of Ramsden. So, as long as you live in Ramsden, I have every right to do whatever it takes to run this town the best I see fit." He gave her a look as if falling in love made a person stupid. "Now if you'll excuse me, I'd like to enjoy what's left of my Sunday."

He left, leaving her standing in the middle of the kitchen, stumped. Picking up the envelope of money her pa had left behind, she recalled what her mother had said about being squeezed out of a man's love.

"You can love a man until your heart is so full of him that it feels like it's going to burst. You can even give him everything a woman can give a man, but if he's got something else in his heart, eventually it's going to shove you right out."

She tossed the envelope aside and threw her shawl over her shoulders. She had to talk to Nate and it was easier to grow a foot taller than to change Zachariah's mind. But Clayton, the part-time deputy, was a pushover. And fortunately Zachariah had returned her horse, which Clayton had borrowed.

Sure enough, Clayton was sitting behind the sheriff's desk. And sure enough, all it took to get Clayton to stand outside the door so she could talk to Nate privately was a pout and a voice full of honey.

But she wasn't so sweet to Nate when he brought his face to the bars. Instead of a kiss, she gave him a tongue-lashing. "Going to a man's home and scaring his family was a foolish thing to do, Nate."

It was the first time she'd ever seen him this unkempt with his coat torn, his shirt soiled, and his hair messed. He pushed away from the bars and paced like a restless coyote in his cell. "I did it because he told you where I'd been. He had no right to tell you."

"Tell me what? What I should have figured out for myself a long time ago? Who took care of you while you were stuck in your melancholy? Who stood by your bedside?"

He stopped pacing, and his eyes softened. "You did, Hattie. So how could you possibly think I was with another woman all that time?"

"Because when you'd gotten engaged to Lillian, you hurt me badly."

"I never loved her. It's always been you, Hattie. You're the only woman who's ever been in my heart."

"Yes." She looked deeply into his eyes as she finally understood what had always come between them. "The only *woman*."

He frowned at her. "You say that with doubt."

"No. I said it with certainty." Although it wasn't a woman, there was someone else in Nate's heart.

"You know my heart belongs to you, so what's the problem? Come with me on tomorrow's stagecoach. That two-bit sheriff can force me to leave Ramsden, but he can't force you to stay."

"I'm not leaving Ramsden, Nate."

"What?" He walked up to the bars that stood between them. "You know I can't stay here."

"Look Nate. I know how much Sally meant to you, but you forget she also meant a lot to Zachariah. He didn't kill her. You didn't kill her. Sally's headstrong nature killed her."

He pushed away from the bars. "Don't go there with me, Hattie."

"If I can't 'go there' with you, how could you expect me to 'go' with you to Massachusetts?"

He stressed each word, "You don't know the whole story between Zachariah and me."

"Then don't you think it's about time you tell me everything?"

"Don't you think it's about time you trust me?"

"Trust you?" She snorted. "That's exactly what our

problem is. You downright shattered my trust in you a long time ago, and moving to Massachusetts won't fix it. You want me to go to a place I've never been, packed with people I've never met who may not accept me, and that leaves me depending solely on you."

"What's wrong with that?"

"Did you hear a word I said, Nate?"

"You want trust? I'll give you every penny I have."

She threw her hands up. "Why does everybody think my hurts can be fixed with money? Dollar bills are just pieces of paper that a good gust of wind can blow away. I need something with substance. I need to trust you again."

"Then *trust* me again. I *know* I was wrong. I *admit* I was wrong. I *regret* it. I'm *sorry*. What more do you want from me?"

"I want you to fix what broke my trust in you in the first place. I want you to make amends with Zachariah, because that's what's keeping me from having everything I love." She pleaded, "You two were friends once—"

"Are you blind?" He threw his hands up. "Look where I am. He put me in jail, Hattie."

She heated at his sarcasm. "No, Nate, I am not blind. Not in the least. And seeing you're behind bars makes me speculate you just might be in jail because the sheriff put you there for good reason."

He huffed repentantly. "I didn't mean to mock you. But my dealings with that hired hand have nothing to do with you."

She stared at him. He couldn't be any more wrong. "Your hatred toward Zachariah has *everything* to do with me.

"And how exactly is that?"

"Your hatred toward Zachariah is keeping you from loving me the way I need you to." She crossed her hands over her chest, yearning for him to understand. "I need you to love me with a whole heart."

"But I do love you. With all my heart."

"No, you don't. Can't you see? You weren't in love with Lillian, but you were still going to marry her because of your hatred toward Zachariah. Zachariah's in your heart, Nate, and your hatred toward him is stronger than your love is for me, and it's shoving me clear out. There's not enough room inside of you for me and all that hatred you have for him. I need you to love me more than you hate Zachariah."

"I do love you more than I hate him."

"Then prove it. Ask Zachariah to forgive you."

"Forgive me! For what?"

"For blaming him for Sally's death. For what you did to Lillian. I know it was you who set that fire. You've got to ask his forgiveness for all the wrongs you've done to him, because you've done him plenty."

His gaze hardened on her. "You're asking too much of me."

"Too much of *you*?" Her hands fell limp to her sides. "What about me, Nate?"

"It's simple." He whispered, "Come with me to Massachusetts. It's the only way we can be together."

Tears welled in her eyes. Her mother had been right all along about Nate having a divided heart. Hattie had always imagined love of money as the potential adversary. But it was hatred.

His hatred for Zachariah was more powerful than his love for her.

"No," she said at last. "You're asking too much of me. If you can't love me with a whole heart, then I can't give you my all, either." She choked. "Good-bye Nate."

26

"Hattie." Nate clutched the bars of his cell. "Don't go." He tried to shake them loose so he could get out and chase after her, but they were as immovable as she was deaf to his plea. "Hattie, come back. Hattie."

Just as she opened the door to leave, Zachariah shot in. He stopped short at the sight of her and cast a scowl at Nate. "If this weren't an emergency, Hattie…"

Clayton stood in the open doorway. "What's wrong?"

"We got big trouble," Zachariah said. "Someone came by my house and left me this."

Clayton's eyes skimmed the note Zachariah handed him. "This isn't good. Who left it?"

"I got no idea. There was a knock at my door, and in the few seconds it took for me to answer, all I saw was the rider's dust."

Hattie moved to Zachariah's side. "What does the note say?"

Zachariah answered, "Krugar Gang's on their way here, and whoever left this note anticipates they'll be here tomorrow around noon."

"What do you think they want?" Clayton asked.

"Probably coming for their Reverend." Nate smirked, knowing his comment wouldn't be appreciated.

"That's enough out of you, Nate," Zachariah said. Then he answered Clayton, "They'll likely want to rob the bank."

"Got a plan?" Clayton asked.

"Not yet. But I reckon we'll be needing as many men as we can get," Zachariah said.

"I'll rustle them up," Clayton said. "But you're the only one who's handy with a rifle, Zachariah. You'll have to hide and pick them off while the rest of us keep them busy shooting."

You fools don't know what you're up against. The fact that the gang was wanted everywhere from Kansas to Texas meant that no one had yet outgunned or outsmarted them. The leader, whoever he was, knew what he was doing.

Nate walked away from the bars and kicked back on the bed, glad this wasn't his problem. In fact, he'd be gone before it even happened, since he was leaving on the morning stagecoach. He folded his hands behind his head and cast a smirk at Zachariah. The man, deep in thought, looked as if he would have to earn his wages.

"And you think they'll not shoot back and kill some of you?" Hattie asked. "There's a better way."

"And what way is that?" Zachariah asked.

"I kept one of my old dresses," Hattie said, tightening her shawl around her.

Nate didn't like the sound of that. He sat up.

"I can distract them," Hattie said. "They're just men. I'm sure I've handled worse."

Nate threw himself off the bed. Using Hattie to distract this gang of killers suddenly made this his problem. "You can't do this, Hattie. These men are killers. I saw them shoot a man."

"What?" Zachariah shot back at Nate. "Why didn't you tell me about this?"

"Well, Zachariah," Nate said sarcastically, "I know you think mighty highly of yourself, but I didn't think you were high and mighty enough to heal a man with a gunshot wound. I brought him to the doctor that first night I was in town and let him handle it. Haven't seen the man since. I assume he left town as soon as he was able to get away from the gang."

"Nate!" Hattie exclaimed.

"Stay out of this. It's not your responsibility." Nate growled.

"He's right," Clayton said.

But Hattie was too bullheaded to listen. "No, Nate, you stay out of this."

Nate turned to Zachariah and demanded, "You're the sheriff. You have no business putting her life on the line."

"He's right," Zachariah said to Hattie.

For the first time since they were children, Nate and Zachariah agreed on something.

But the two of them teaming up against Hattie only caused her to fire back at Nate. "Mind your business and let me mind mine."

Then she spouted the specifics of her plans to Zachariah. Plans about distracting the gang on their way into town. Plans that Zachariah didn't seem to like.

Nate wasn't listening to her for another moment. "The only thing she'll lure the Krugar Gang into doing is killing her."

"Don't listen to him," Hattie said to Zachariah. "I can do this. I know I can."

"And I know you can't," Nate said.

Hattie growled at him. "This is *our* business."

Nate pleaded with her, "It's just money."

"No, Nate, it's the *town's* money," Hattie said. "These people worked hard for every cent of it. So I'm doing this for the people I love. I'm doing this for Ramsden."

"You just told me that money can't fix what hurts you, so why are you risking your life for it?" Nate said. "Zachariah, don't listen to her. She's crazy."

The room went quiet, until Hattie broke the silence. "I owe everything to this town." She glanced from Clayton to Zachariah and then glared at Nate. "And I owe him nothing. I'll be in front of the saloon at eleven o'clock sharp, Zachariah." She tore her gaze off Nate and closed the door hard behind her.

"Don't do it, Hattie!" Nate tugged at the accursed bars. "You'll get yourself killed!"

27

Monday morning brought Hattie back to her usual chores but in a hollow way. After returning from Kate's, she succumbed to slumping in a chair and crying, knowing that with each passing minute a stagecoach was taking Nate further away. But she had to pull herself together. She had another thing to do today.

She drew the red dress Nate had given her years ago out of her trunk and clutched it close. She could never get rid of it, not because it was such a fine and fancy dress, but because Nate had given it to her. *If only you knew what love was.*

She bit her lip. What love meant for her was that Zachariah, Clayton, and the whole town could count on her. If only they fully realized what she was giving up for them.

She couldn't look in the mirror as she peeled off the modest calico dress of a virtuous woman and slipped into the off-the-shoulder-dress of the saloon girl she'd left behind.

Lord, I don't want to do this.

She didn't want to stand in front of the saloon. She didn't want to be a floozy again, flirting with dirty men. She didn't want old folks to remember what she was and new folks to learn about her past. But most of all, she didn't want to be anywhere near Boss, who'd beat her and imprisoned her—and still scared her half to death.

But Zachariah, her guardian angel, would take care of her. Wouldn't he?

She pulled her hair down from its bun. Forcing herself to face the mirror, she draped her hair over her shoulder and brushed the black tresses until they shone, and there she was once again. Hard-as-nails Hattie Brown.

She felt fragile as glass.

You may look it on the outside, but in your heart, you're not that woman any more. The Lord's voice spoke to her, assured her.

She was a woman with a higher purpose and that purpose involved stopping a gang from hurting anyone in her town. She'd handled cantankerous men and rowdies who liked to pick fights. But could she handle outlaws? Outright killers?

Did Nate really see them shoot a man and leave him for dead? He wasn't exactly reliable, was he? He was so adamant about her not getting involved.

But she had to prove to him how much this town meant to her. Or maybe she was deeply drawn into trying to prove to herself what Nate *didn't* mean to her. Whatever the reason, she was now in it up to her neck, and it was time to go. Everyone was counting on her. On her way out the door, she spotted the money envelope her father had left her and snatched it up. She'd best give it to Zachariah, just in case Nate was right.

~*~

Nate looked out the window of the stagecoach at the passing scrub. He was tired and sore from what had turned out to be a futile struggle with Zachariah, but most of all, he was worried about Hattie.

Hoping to escape so he could stop her from carrying out her plan, he'd fought with all his might from boarding the stagecoach. "You're supposed to be the sheriff," he'd shouted at Zachariah. "You should be doing your job and not having a woman do it for you. You'll get her killed."

But Zachariah had outmuscled him, bound his hands and feet, and forced him inside the stagecoach. Zachariah had even saddled his horse and escorted the stagecoach until Nate was well out of town.

Nate was so consumed with Hattie's role in their harebrained plan to capture the gang that he hadn't even thought of saying good-bye to his mother, but Zachariah remembered and promised to do it for him. Was Nate supposed to be grateful to him?

And now Nate was so far away from Ramsden that even if he could turn the stagecoach around, he'd never get back in time to stop Hattie from taking part in their crazy plan. And that took the last ounce of struggle out of him. "Hey," he shouted to the driver. "Think you can take these ropes off me now?"

The stagecoach stopped, and a man who wasn't the driver came down and approached the window. "I'll untie you on condition you promise to act like a gentleman."

Hattie's father?

Did he know what Hattie was up to? Not likely, and there was no reason to worry the man by telling him about something neither of them could stop.

"There's no need to fight anymore." Nate offered his bound wrists.

"Good," Parker said. "Because you were, shall I

say, a bit quarrelsome with the sheriff, which is why I sat outside with the driver, until such time as you decided to settle down. Personally, I'd rather be sitting in here where the seat is softer." He called to the driver, "I'll keep an eye on him" and then climbed inside.

After untying Nate, Parker sat opposite him. "As I recall, you were the man I saw at the eatery with Miss Hattie," Parker said. "Might you be courting her?"

"I thought I might have been, but it looks as though she has other plans that don't include me." Nate shook off the tingling in his hands.

"I'm afraid I'm sitting in the same stagecoach because her plans don't include me, either," Parker said.

"Seems I can't give her what she wants."

"Which is?"

"She claims I don't love her enough, but I do, Mr. Parker."

"Well, Mister–"

"Nathan Powell. Call me Nate." They shook hands.

"Well, Nate, if you indeed love her as much as you say you do, then you'd be a fool to leave her. So, why are you, son? What happened between you?"

"What happened is that she's too hardheaded." Nate checked his chain watch and then rubbed his jaw. It was almost twelve o'clock. If he was a praying man, he'd be praying for her now. Zachariah had better take good care of her. "She wouldn't come back with me to Massachusetts."

Parker frowned. "Massachusetts?"

"That's where I live, and I'm well-established."

"She seemed mighty content to live in Ramsden,"

Parker said. "Everyone seemed to know her there and think well of her."

Well enough to put her in danger. "Perhaps you noticed," Nate said, "that the sheriff and I don't get along well."

"I did, son. But I couldn't help thinking it was more like you not getting along well with him. He *is* the sheriff."

Nate snorted. "He's nothing but a two-bit hired hand who happens to be taller than everyone else."

"So that's why they made him sheriff?" Parker smiled.

Had they not been talking about Zachariah, Nate might have returned the smile.

"If I may impart upon you the hard-earned wisdom of an older man, I might say that I also heard how you spoke to him. You think you're better than he is. No person is better than another, and our Lord proved that's a fact because He died for us all, regardless."

Nate turned to the window and the view of brown grass and bushes outside. "I hope you won't preach at me all the way to Kansas."

"No, I'm won't, but if you'll bear with a man of regret one moment longer, I will lecture you on the love of a fine woman. You see, son, sometimes there's one special lady who graces a man's path during his lifetime. A woman whose love is as soft as a rose petal and as solid as an oak. And if you let something else you think is more important stop you from having her, before you know it, a lifetime's over, and you find yourself with no memories of holding her in your arms in your bed at night or saying grace at mealtimes with the children she has borne you. All you're left with is the emptiness of what could have been." His gray-blue eyes clouded over. "If God has offered her to you, then nothing of this world is worth giving her up for, son. Nothing." Parker blew his nose and stayed silent for a time.

Nate felt the emptiness suggested in Parker's words.

The horses ahead stirred clouds of dust as the two men looked away from each other and let the stiff stagecoach joggle and jolt their spiritless bodies.

Then, something outside the window caught Parker's attention, and he straightened. "If you'll excuse me, son, but you wouldn't happen to have a pistol on you, would you?"

That was a ridiculous question, considering the circumstances.

"No."

"Then," Parker said, "I suspect we're about to be robbed."

~*~

Hattie stood in front of the saloon, knowing Boss was watching her from the window.

He had nothing to do with the plan, just the displeasure of it taking place in front of his business where a stray bullet might bust a window, or worse, his precious mirror.

She could feel the heat of Boss's eyes on her, coveting her body, wanting to possess her soul once again. Though she felt faint, she held her head straight, looking strong for Zachariah. She caught a glimpse of him on the rooftop of the telegraph office. Clayton's shape was behind the curtain in the sheriff's office.

There were five other men hiding behind doors and in alleys nearby, merchants, blacksmiths, men who barely knew how to pull a trigger. The Reverend was nowhere to be found. *Thank goodness for that.* He'd once told her he was opposed to guns and that was a good thing, because he was so butterfingered, guns were likely even more opposed to him.

Ramsden was as well prepared as it could be for the Krugar Gang.

Hattie fanned herself with her hand. It wasn't so much the heat as it was her nerves.

Then Zachariah raised his rifle over his head. That was the signal. It was time to sway her hips.

Though she didn't take pride in it, strutting in a way she'd once mastered came back easily. Every man she'd encountered in her years working at the saloon had been easily diverted with that walk, and once distracted, they became dumber than dirt. She'd send them an inviting smile, breathe some sweet talk in their ears, and pickpocket their guns. Easy as pie.

Just hopefully not the kind of pies she made.

Hooves pounded the earth and sent the dust swirling as the gang started down Main Street. While her hips swayed, her heart thundered.

Killers.

But the odds were in her favor of catching their fancies, since there weren't many women in these parts. Especially women who looked like her.

Four riders, cocky as roosters ready for the butcher's ax, were riding into her trap.

She cast a glance at Zachariah. *We can do this. I know we can.*

The front rider reached Hattie and came to a halt but signaled the others to keep going. She'd hoped they all would have stopped, so why hadn't they? When the rider got down from the horse and approached Hattie, she got her answer. She was in a lot of trouble.

This person was the last one Hattie expected to encounter.

~*~

A shot rang out, and the stagecoach came to a jarring halt.

"Hands in the air." A masked man yelled.

Neither Nate nor Parker had a pistol to fight back. They looked up to the driver.

"He shot it right out of my hand," the driver said.

All three raised their hands.

The outlaw unhitched a horse from the stagecoach and led it beside his own. He pointed to the driver and Parker. "You and you, back on the stagecoach." He smacked the still hitched horse so it took off running, taking the stagecoach. He pointed at Nate. "You're coming with me."

"Now listen," Nate started, but the man interrupted him.

"There's no time for this." He tugged off his cover.

Nate's jaw dropped. "Cadwell?"

Cadwell tied a rope around the neck of the horse. "Since you already know about me, and no one believes you anyway, I need your help."

"What kind of help do you possibly think I'd want to give you?" Nate asked.

"The kind that will benefit us both." Cadwell mounted the horse, bareback. "Hattie's been captured by Joe Krugar."

28

The horse beneath Nate was swift. In no time he'd caught up to Cadwell, whose horse chopped up the dry grass with its hooves. Bareback riding at this speed proved Cadwell was an excellent horseman. Shooting, acting...was there anything this man couldn't do well?

"Who are you?" Nate asked.

"It doesn't matter who I am. All that matters is that I'm on your side," Cadwell answered. "For the time being, anyway."

"And what exactly does your alliance entail?" Nate asked.

"I have my own agenda, but right now what I want just happens to coincide with what you want. I take it you *do* want to get Hattie out of her present situation?" Cadwell looked toward Nate for an answer.

"Of course I do."

"Then let me fill you in on what I know, and I'd appreciate you not wasting time by asking how I know it." It took some concentration on Cadwell's part, but he rode impressively well bareback at a full run.

Nate would have fallen off at this speed.

"When I learned the gang was coming to Ramsden, I left a note warning the sheriff and recommending he evacuate everyone from the main street and let the gang go ahead and rob the bank. I was afraid it might escalate into a shootout, with no one left standing but the gang. I planned to catch up to the gang on the outskirts of town and get the money back, and that should have been the end of it."

Cadwell's recommendations to the town left Nate again questioning Cadwell's affiliation with the gang—and whether cooperating with him was a wise idea. "Interesting plan," Nate said.

When he'd been in the jailhouse, Zachariah had mentioned nothing about letting the gang rob the bank. Why would Zachariah leave that part out?

Nate knew why. "Zachariah's not one to back down," he admitted.

"Apparently neither is Hattie," Cadwell added. "Good woman." He cast a long glance at Nate, making a point.

"I told her not to get involved in this," Nate said.

"What exactly was she trying to do?" Cadwell said.

"Use her feminine wiles to outsmart the gang." He gave a shake of his head. "She could charm her way into snatching a gun right out of a man's hand. I've seen her do it back when she worked in the saloon." The part about the saloon had slipped. But then again, the man riding beside him was no saint, either.

"What she tried to do was courageous," Cadwell said. "And a woman as beautiful as she is all dressed up?" He gave a smile of appreciation at the thought. "It might have distracted the men, but it wouldn't have worked on Joe."

Nate eyed the man riding alongside him. No one even knew what Joe Krugar, the gang's leader, looked like because no one could get a picture of him. Not even a sketch. But Cadwell talked about him as if he knew him personally. "You seem awfully familiar with him."

"With her," Cadwell said. "That's Joe, as in Josephine."

That morsel of information took a minute for Nate to digest. "The leader of the Krugar Gang is a woman?"

"The most unscrupulous lady I've ever encountered."

The word "unscrupulous" to describe any outlaw, whether man or woman, agreed with Nate, but "lady" was another matter. For Cadwell to have called her one suggested his acquaintance with her was more than casual. "Care to tell me what you know about her?"

"She's dangerous, she's cunning, and that's everything you need to know." Cadwell's bluntness suggested that was all the information Nate was going to get.

"What do you suspect she'll do with Hattie?"

"I suspect Josephine's going to use her as leverage."

That wasn't a good thing to hear, but what Nate asked next was even worse. "Why would she put so much stock into a saloon girl?"

"Josephine's not stupid," Cadwell said. "She's figured out that Hattie's role in all this was staged and that she's valuable to the town." He turned to Nate. "This wasn't a very good plan. I wished they'd have listened to me."

Nate kept from spouting out his agreement.

In no time, the outskirts of Ramsden came into view.

Cadwell tied the covering back over his face. "I'll need my horse."

It was a peculiar mask, and Nate couldn't help staring at it for a moment before surrendering the animal.

Cadwell mounted.

"You'll have to walk from here," Cadwell said. "I'll slip the horse we commandeered back into the livery so it can go back to its rightful owner next time the stagecoach is back in town. I hope you can come up with a good plan to get Hattie back. It'll be a challenge to outsmart Josephine. She's already outsmarted the sheriff. Which, by the way," Cadwell added, savvy to Nate's opportunity to gloat, "you shouldn't be too smug about. Josephine's getting the upper hand this time, since she's been outfoxing sheriffs, Texas Rangers, bounty hunters, and even U.S. Marshals for eight years now."

"She must be quite a lady," Nate said.

The odd cover over Cadwell's face, with only his eyes peering out, covered up his response.

"Speaking of better plans," Nate said, staring at Cadwell's mask. "Is that a doily you're wearing over your face?"

"It's a—dresser scarf," Cadwell said. "I didn't want anyone to recognize me, and—it was the only thing handy at the spur of the moment."

Had Hattie not been in danger, Nate would have had a good laugh. "You look like a harem girl."

"I'll find something that looks a bit more—intimidating—in the future. Godspeed, Nate." He was about to ride off but turned. "There's one thing I want you to do for me."

"And that is?"

"Do whatever it takes to get Hattie back. But as for Josephine, leave the little vixen for me." He spurred the horse and was off.

~*~

A long walk into town allowed Nate to clear his mind. Even if he didn't have a plan, he had a destination.

The sheriff's office was crowded with six uneasy men.

A pacing Zachariah stopped short when Nate entered. "What are you doing back here?"

Nate would do whatever it took to rescue Hattie, even if it meant eating crow from Zachariah. But Nate could serve some up as well. "I'm here to get Hattie back, since you failed so miserably to protect her. I warned you about that gang. How could you let this happen to her?"

"She's my concern, not yours," Zachariah barked.

"Strong words," Nate retorted, "for a hired hand."

"No, Nate." In an unusual fit of rage, Zachariah barged toward him. "Strong words for a sheriff. And don't you forget that. But most of all—" He thumped his chest, his face in Nate's. "—don't you forget you're not the only one who cares about Hattie."

"We're all worried about her, Nate," Clayton said.

The other men chimed in, diverting Nate's attention away from Zachariah.

"Nobody can figure out what to do," Clayton said. "We're at our wit's end, and time's running out. Got any ideas?"

Nate reeled in his temper. "What do you mean time's running out?"

"The gang left a message with the Reverend that we got until five o'clock this evening to bring them the money. If we don't, they're threatening to kill Hattie."

The words made Nate's heart race. Consulting his

watch brought him close to a panic. "It's past four o'clock now." How was he supposed to come up with a plan *and* implement it in less than an hour? If only Zachariah hadn't sent him away...

Nate wanted to lunge at him. And then what? Get held down by a half-dozen men and end up in jail again where he'd be no use at all to Hattie?

He had to think rationally not emotionally. And thinking rationally began by swallowing an unsavory helping of humble pie. Nate needed to be filled in on everything. He turned to Zachariah. "All right, Sheriff." Saying that didn't taste as bad as he thought it might. "Let's begin by you telling me everything you know."

"First of all," Zachariah said, "I want to know how you found out she'd been captured and how you got back here."

Discussing Cadwell's puzzling dual identity wasn't an option, as past efforts had already proven it futile. "What does it matter how I found out?" Nate had to get Zachariah's feet on the same road. "Fifty minutes doesn't give us enough time for a hundred questions. So let's try this again." Sensibly spelling it out to Zachariah also helped Nate to get a foothold on his patience with the man—and to stay focused on what needed to be done. "For me to come up with a big plan in so little time in order to save Hattie's life, I need you to tell me what you know." There. He'd spelled it out, urgency and all, clear as spring water.

Zachariah clamped his jaw and then relaxed it for an uneasy truce. "We spotted four riders, three men, one might have been a boy."

Nate kept it to himself that the "boy" was Josephine.

"We closed the businesses and cleared the streets," Zachariah said.

Nate didn't say anything but noted the "closed" sign hanging across the street on a door in the middle of the day probably tipped Josephine off that the town knew they were coming. Yet another mistake in this chain of catastrophes.

"Since we wanted to capture them, we didn't want to start firing and scare them off, so we waited for Hattie to do her part. She was standing in front of the saloon, and the next thing we knew…" Zachariah hesitated. "They had her."

Easy as that? It was hard to believe, because Hattie was a fighter. "They may have out-muscled her onto a horse," Nate said. "But how'd they keep her from jumping off?"

Zachariah swallowed. "They knocked her out cold."

Nate wanted to punch the daylights out of Zachariah. But he clenched his teeth and paced instead.

"The gang went between the buildings, riding single file, but they put Hattie on the last horse, so I couldn't get a clear shot at them. Not without risking hitting her. They fired a few rounds and hit Malachi. He'll be all right. He's with Doc. Right now we're getting together a posse."

"A posse of what?" Nate said. "Merchants, blacksmiths, and a telegrapher? You'll have a half-dozen fledglings firing at Hattie. No offense, Clayton."

"None taken," Clayton said. "He's right, Zachariah. You're the only one here handy with a rifle."

"So what do you propose we do?" Zachariah asked, his gaze on Nate. "They want us to bring ten thousand dollars to the ravine. We can't come up with that kind of money."

That amount raised Nate's brow, initially with the shock of the amount—and then with an easy solution to the problem. "I have the money at my bank."

Clayton perked. "I can wire it in." He shot out the door toward the telegraph office with Nate following.

Ten minutes later, Nate told Clayton to stop tapping away at the telegraph. "There's nobody at the bank. It closes at five, and—"

"And Boston's ahead of our time." Clayton threw up his hands.

It was back to the sheriff's office but with ten minutes wasted. The men inside were discussing the problem.

"There's four of them and six of us. I'd say we just go after them."

"In that ravine?"

"They'll not be *in* the ravine, they'll be hiding somewhere along the top."

"And that's the problem. We'll never find them. The ravine's a good mile and a half long. It's full of places for them to hide. They'll gun every one of us down."

"But what else can we do? We've got to at least put up a fight, because if we can't give them what they want, then Hattie's good as—"

"Don't say it." Standing at the doorway, Nate was compelled to speak up. "Maybe if we can get Tilly to cooperate just a little…"

"How little?" Zachariah said.

"Ten thousand dollars' worth?" Nate asked. "A loan. I'll pay him back myself."

"It's no use," Zachariah said. "He wants no part of

this, and we've already wasted the better part of the afternoon trying to talk him into it."

"If he wasn't the only banker in town," Clayton said, "he'd have no part of me."

"Me, neither," the others agreed.

"So all we've got is what's in our accounts as well as what's under our hats, and it doesn't even add up to a thousand dollars," Clayton said. "Wait a minute." His wrinkled brow creased more as he walked behind the desk. "Hattie dropped something off this morning for me to give to Zachariah to hold on to. I suspected it might be some money, so I put it in the drawer, and with everything going on..." He retrieved a sealed envelope and handed it to Zachariah.

Hattie knew the plan would be dangerous, so why did she go ahead and do it? That was another dart to throw at Zachariah, but they had to stick to the matter at hand. "Even if it is all her money, how much can she possibly have?"

"Won't hurt to check." Zachariah opened the envelope and fanned two stacks of legal tender notes with Ben Franklin's face on them. "It's full of hundreds." He counted the money. "She's got two thousand dollars here."

"Where'd she get that kind of money?" Clayton asked.

"I'm guessing her father gave it to her before he left," Zachariah said.

"That's a lot of money." The other men's faces filled with hope that Zachariah snuffed out.

"It's still not ten thousand dollars."

Nate rubbed his jaw. "Two thousand might still be enough."

"If we give them less than they want, we'll put her

in danger," Zachariah said.

"So will doing nothing," Clayton added.

But Nate kept rubbing his jaw. Time was ticking away fast and with no plan and being short of money...could the scheme work? Could he outsmart the notorious Josephine Krugar?

He checked his watch. Thirty-five minutes left to go. They just might have enough time and resources to pull it off. "We may not have enough money, but you've got paper in this town, don't you?"

Clayton's eyes lit up. "Now that's something we happen to have plenty of."

"Why?" Zachariah straightened in his chair. "What do you have in mind?"

"If we can't outgun them, and we can't give them what they want," Nate said, "we'll have to outwit them."

29

Hattie gained consciousness on the dirt floor of a musty mine, her head throbbing. She sat up, touched the tender spot on her head, and discovered it was wet and sticky because it was bleeding.

"She's awake now," said a ferret-like voice. "Want me to tie her up?"

"You're a little too eager, Mel. I'll do it myself." The second voice was slow and businesslike, and it gave Hattie goosebumps.

A rusty lantern illuminated a tall man with a bony face and shadows beneath his eyes. Hattie shielded her eyes from the brightness as he carried the lantern over to her. He reeled her around with undue roughness and tied her wrists behind her back with an itchy rope. Two men scurried up like rodents to ogle the creamy mounds that her low-cut dress boasted.

"We got plans for you," Mel said to Hattie, and then he grinned with brown-crusted teeth. The other man was even uglier, with a spray of thin hair, patchy beard, and greedy eyes. They both stank like polecats.

A slight figure wearing a man's shirt and trousers, belt cinched in at the waist showing an hourglass figure, stepped into the light. She pushed back a lock of flaxen hair from her ivory face and exposed her ice-gray eyes.

How did I get here? Hattie remembered strutting in

front of the saloon, hanging onto her nerve as four riders rode up and one stopped, and looking up to find that the face beneath the hat was a woman's. Oh, yes. And meeting, up close and personal, the butt of her rifle.

"A woman as beautiful as you can handle any *man*, can't she?" The woman had snatched the idea out of Hattie's head but spoke with elocution as fine as Nate's. "Mel and Bill, stop gawking at her."

Mel started, "But she's just a—"

"You say that word, and I will personally carve out your tongue." Her voice was a tranquil river—a trickling, almost melodic flow—but her eyes were a tempest. "Tom, get these dolts away from her."

The two polecats scurried away before Tom had a chance to oblige.

Storm-cloud eyes stayed on Hattie as the woman approached. Though she wore trousers and a plaid shirt, she moved with the poise of a lady carrying a parasol and wearing the finest of dresses.

"My name is Josephine. What's yours?"

Hattie didn't answer, because she saw in the beautiful face that this was the calm before a storm. Instead, she prayed for strength.

"Pretty." Josephine knelt by Hattie's side and, with soft fingertips, turned Hattie's face toward hers. As beautiful as Hattie was, this woman was her blonde equal. "*Very* pretty. But you're no *fille de joie*. I can tell by your eyes. You don't have that hard look. So, who are you?"

Hattie jerked away. "I'm nobody."

"Oh, you're precious to someone. So I'll call you Pearl." Josephine's voice was smooth as the satin ribbon that pulled back her wavy hair. "A woman doesn't just waste away by herself in a town full of men. He must have been worth your while, rich—" Her cold eyes found the scars on Hattie's arms. "—and mean." She turned her back to Hattie and lowered the shoulder of her shirt to show several welts, like red earthworms, healed into her back. "But I've got some scars of my own, so don't expect any sympathy from me, dearest." She buttoned her shirt. "But the worst scars are the ones a man leaves on your heart. Have you ever been in love, Pearl?" Perhaps, as Josephine spoke in a dreamy voice, she hungered for female company.

"Haven't we all?" The rope cutting off the circulation in Hattie's hands was a good reminder she was *captive* female company.

"What was yours like?" Josephine asked as though they were sipping tea together.

"Like yours, I reckon."

"You 'reckon'? How charming." Josephine came to her full height, slim, stately, and thoroughly out of sorts with the homely men. "There never was, nor will there ever be, a man like Jake." Her eyes softened, but hardened again. "So my question is, is your 'somebody' ten thousand dollars' worth of rich?" Josephine sighed at the blankets and pans strewn beneath the beams and the cobwebs. "I'm tired of living in places like this." She nodded toward the men. "And with vermin like that. And as for you, pretty Pearl, I'm sure you'd like to live." Two storm cloudy eyes, heavy with thunder and hail about to break lose, lingered on Hattie.

And a torrent would erupt from this woman, because all the people left in Hattie's life could never come up with that much money. "Nate," she groaned.

Josephine's interest roused. "Who's this Nate?" It would destroy Nate if he ever knew what became of her. "My 'somebody.'"

"So you do—"

"And my Jake." Hattie added, "So you'll not get one red cent for me."

Josephine's heart-shaped lips curled at the edges. "Well, let's play this hand out anyway." She laid light fingers on Hattie's shoulder. "I'm willing to take bets on you, Pearl." Josephine's voice became terse. "Tom, you *did* deliver the ransom note. Am I correct?"

"I had Mel do it."

Josephine shot him a gaze. "I told you to do it."

"I thought you—"

"I didn't tell you to think, I told you to do, because the last time you 'thought,' you brought back a couple of men who have the intelligence of two mules. If I had wanted Mel to do it, I would have told Mel to do it."

"Mel ain't that stupid," Tom said. "And I didn't want to chance getting caught."

Josephine snorted a laugh. "Apparently I gave Mel more credit than his intelligence warrants. And you put that kind of responsibility on him?"

Mel whined, "I delivered the note. Tom said to leave it at some business, so I left it over at the church."

"You left it at the *church*?" Josephine's voice arched. "I wanted someone to find it *today*. People only go to church on Sundays. You're not only a heathen, you're a fool."

Mel spurted, "But I saw a preacher inside. I'm sure he found it."

"For your sake, he'd better have." Josephine covered her hair and the ribbon with a fedora. "All right, boys. It's time to go." She looked down at Hattie.

"Pearl, you're riding with me." Again, the butt of Josephine's rifle smashed into Hattie's head.

30

"Whew." Clayton waved a hand in front of his face to shoo away an odor. "They sure smell strong. And they look too neat. It wouldn't convince me one bit."

It didn't convince Nate either, but they'd run out of time and there were no other options. "This will have to do," Nate said.

The items of interest were ten packets Zachariah had just brought in to the sheriff's office and spilled onto the desk. Each bundle consisted of a one hundred-dollar bill on top, one on the bottom, and eight pieces of paper cut to like size in between.

Clayton picked up a stack and tried to fan them. "They stick," he said.

"So does money fresh off the press," Nate said. But the papers in between were lime green and damp from the dye Kate had concocted out of vegetable greens and vinegar. Hence the smell.

"Maybe it'll help if we make this look more official," Nate said. "Do you think Tilly might at least loan us some banker's bags?"

Clayton started to protest. "He said he won't have anything to do with this whole matter."

But Zachariah said, "Hanged if he won't," and shot out the door. In no time, Zachariah returned with empty banker's bags in one hand and Tilly by the scruff of the collar in the other. Zachariah shoved Tilly toward the desk. "You want this in your bank?"

Tilly's eyes grew wide. "Where'd you get all this money?" Apparently, Zachariah hadn't told him all the particulars—especially the one where they weren't planning on getting it back. "And why does it smell like…" Tilly sniffed. "Vinegar?"

"Time's run out," Zachariah said. "Give us the bags." Even though he was strong-arming Tilly, Zachariah would never take anything without permission.

Tilly yielded, and the rest of the men shoved the money into the bags.

The question that lingered now was who would deliver it to the Krugar Gang. There was only Zachariah, Clayton, Nate, and Tilly left standing in the sheriff's office.

Tilly read the question on everyone's faces and abruptly left.

"I'll do it," Clayton said. But his hands shook when he picked up one of the bags and betrayed his lack of confidence.

If the Krugar Gang suspected they were being hoodwinked, they'd examine the money closely, and not only would it be all over for Hattie, but for the messenger as well.

"It's my plan," Nate said. "I'll do it."

"It's my fault Hattie's in this mess," Zachariah said. "I'll do it."

"There's no time to argue." Nate grabbed the bags and thrust them into the saddlebags of the closest horse. "You're the better rifleman, Zachariah, and you need to do what you do best. I'll need you to keep a keen eye out for Hattie in case the plan goes sour."

Zachariah offered one of his guns. "You might need this."

Nate tucked it in his belt. "I'm hoping for a nice, clean exchange." He looked squarely at Zachariah. "But if it doesn't work out that way, I don't care about me. You just make sure Hattie gets out of this alive."

Clayton cleared his throat. "Speaking of sour, what will you do about that smell?"

"Get me some more vinegar."

A moment later, Zachariah ran out of the general store carrying a bottle of vinegar and shouting over his shoulder, "I'll pay you for it later." He handed the bottle to Nate, and Nate saturated his clothes with it.

"The money doesn't smell like vinegar. I do."

"I can figure out my part, but we didn't come up with much of a plan. What's the rest of it?" Zachariah asked.

Nate hesitated. Cadwell was the rest of it. A man who could shoot a hole in a man's necktie could play a valuable part.

"The less men, the better," Nate said. "We don't want a shootout; we just want to get Hattie back. The gang can keep the money." Nate swung into the saddle. To ensure Cadwell was indeed there, Nate added, "Clayton, I need you to ride out to the church and tell the Reverend what we're doing."

"The *Reverend*?" Clayton and Zachariah said in unison.

Clayton's open mouth insinuated, *Are you crazy*?

The furrow in Zachariah's brow questioned, *Since when have you gotten religion?*

Nate turned his horse toward the road. "The rest of the plan is a matter of faith." Then he called over his shoulder as he was riding off, "Tell the Reverend we can use some—divine intervention."

Nate raced the horse out of town and toward the ravine. He tried to ignore how strongly he reeked of vinegar and how clever Cadwell had said that Josephine Krugar was. An image of someone striking Hattie and her falling limp onto the boardwalk urged Nate faster. "Giddy up." He wanted to personally dole out justice for the man—or woman—who'd hit her, but as for anyone getting their due, that would be all up to Cadwell. With Nate's plan, the best he could hope for was to get Hattie back alive.

And that was a long shot for anyone with a sense of smell.

When he'd stumbled upon the gang on his way into Ramsden they'd shot a man, thinking they'd killed him, for none other than the sake of killing. That fact made him believe they'd killed in such a way before. The knowledge that Hattie was in the hands of such cold-blooded murderers lashed at Nate. Would they kill her just for the thrill of it?

"Whoa." When he reached the ravine, he looked at his watch and broke into a sweat. Seven minutes late had him worried. How patient was this Josephine? Had the gang come and gone, leaving behind Hattie's body? Best not to think that way. Best to think that Josephine would allow seven minutes for ten thousand dollars.

A narrow valley where the river snaked through had dwindled to a muddy stream. The stubby trees and shrubs along it were few and scraggly, offering no place for him to hide. This wasn't a good place to ride when there were four guns pointing at one man from the many places to hide along the jagged rim.

"You got the money?" A voice came from afar,

and Nate imagined an astute Josephine standing by the man's elbow.

An uneasy feeling about Cadwell crept up. Could Cadwell be part of this very setup? Part of the gang—like the old poster had shown him to be? Had Cadwell gotten Nate only as a means to figure out how to get the money when no one else could? Nate's gut twisted. At the moment, he was putting more of his eggs in Zachariah's basket than in Cadwell's.

Cadwell was too much of a wildcard.

But Nate had taken off in a flurry, leaving Zachariah to find a horse, catch up, and find a place to hide.

"Hey, you got the money?"

So much for stalling.

"Yes, I've got it." Nate's voice echoed. They knew where he was, but he didn't know where they were. Or where they were keeping Hattie.

"You got all the money?" The question returned like a bad omen.

"Of course I've got it all," Nate bluffed. Even if it was "all" of two thousand instead of ten.

"Ride into the ravine about a quarter mile," the voice called. "You'll find a rock that looks like a skull. Bring the money there."

Nate knew the ravine well, because he and Zachariah used to play there as children back when they were friends. "Skull Rock," as they'd called it, was a poorly-shaped oval about two feet wide by three feet high. Furthermore, Tom had given away his position, because the rock looked like a skull only from a particular vantage point. Nate didn't want them to know he knew their position, so he turned and spoke in a different direction. "Show me Hattie first."

"After you bring us the money."

"Fair enough." Nate glanced behind at the saddlebags. The plan didn't seem as good now as it had an hour ago. *Zachariah, I can give you just a little more time to get here. But not much more.* "I'm coming," he called out. Gingerly coaxing the horse down a manageable incline, he made it even more manageable for the horse by zigzagging slowly into the ravine.

"Something wrong with your horse, mister?"

"Just keeping an eye open for snakes," Nate offered. The slope let go of a few loose rocks, but the horse was sure-footed and had no trouble. Finally, Nate reached the floor of the ravine. A path that narrowed down to five feet wide between two sixty-foot walls was an uncomfortable place to be.

The breeze was hot and dry enough to make jerky. Stalling for as much time as he could so Zachariah could get there, Nate walked the horse along the muddy stream that ran through the ravine. Riding through a stretch where the walls on either side of him bulged together tunnel-like, he found he had to duck. He didn't have to do that as a kid. He reached the familiar rock. "I'm here," Nate called.

"Mel," the voice ordered, "make sure he's got the money."

"Tell him to raise his hands first," Mel called from behind the rock.

Nate could see Mel's boots sticking out and lost patience with the fool. "I'm five feet away from you, Mel. I can hear you better than Tom can." Nate raised his hands. "My hands are in the air. You can come out now."

A weasel of a man appeared from behind Skull Rock. He pointed his gun at Nate. "Where's the money?"

Nate inwardly grinned. If his plan worked, Mel was the right man for the job. The horse shifted beneath Nate as he nodded toward its rump. "The money's in that saddlebag."

Gun on Nate, Mel threw open the saddlebag and got a nose full. "Whew! What's that smell?"

"It's me," Nate said. "I spilled some vinegar on my clothes. Here."

Mel sniffed, and then jerked his face away from the saturated sleeve Nate offered. Content, Mel threw open a saddlebag and cut a slit into one of the money bags. He began counting its contents.

"One, two..." Fortunately he counted the stacks and not the bills, until he called to the other man, "How much is supposed to be here?"

"Ten thousand dollars, you halfwit," the voice said. "Is it all there?"

Mel singled out a stack to start counting the finer details.

Nate rushed in. "Look, Mel, you know why that man called you a halfwit?"

Mel responded with a pout that invited Nate down from the horse.

"He called you a halfwit because he would have had it all counted by now. You see, each stack has ten one hundred-dollar bills in it. Ten times one hundred equals a thousand. There are ten stacks in all, so ten times one thousand makes ten thousand. Or you can look at it this way: ten thousand divided by one hundred equals one hundred. Divide one hundred by ten and what do you have?"

Mel's brow wrinkled with the befuddled look Nate had hoped for.

"It leaves you ten, Mel, and you haven't even counted to four yet. It'll take you into next week to count to ten thousand. Do you think that man up there has that kind of patience? Here. Let me make it easier on you." Nate snatched a stack. "Each bundle has ten one hundred-dollar bills in it." Nate showed him the bill on top and then flipped it over to show him the one on the bottom.

"What about the ones in the middle?"

"I just went over that, Mel. It'll take too long to count everything. That's why they're in bundles. Now, I already explained that each bundle is a thousand dollars. Ten bundles equal ten thousand dollars. So if you count just the bundles, you only have to count to ten, and that would leave you with a total of ten thousand dollars."

"What's taking so long," the voice called.

"See how easy that is to understand?" Nate said.

Mel was obliged to save time and dignity by nodding. He took the stack from Nate. "How many bundles do I need?"

"Just ten."

"'Just ten' don't sound like much."

"Mel, let me tell you something. 'Just ten' is a lot of money when they're all hundred-dollar bills."

Mel counted the contents of the money bag and then frowned. "There's only five here."

"Check the other bag." Even though Mel's stupidity was an advantage, it was scraping on Nate's patience.

Mel counted to his satisfaction. "It's all here, Tom," he called.

Nate called out, "Now, give me Hattie."

Mel clutched the bundles of money to his chest,

but he couldn't manage them while keeping a gun on Nate. All but two of the bundles fell, so Mel thrust his gun into its holster and grabbed the money in a way Nate was concerned would break the bands and cause bright green paper to fall out.

"Since you're stealing ten thousand dollars," Nate said, "why don't you steal the saddlebags as well? Might be easier to carry the money in them." Nate hoped Zachariah wouldn't resent losing his gear.

"Put the money in the saddlebags, then," Mel said, pointing his gun at Nate.

Nate did so, and then slung the bags over Mel's shoulder.

"Give me your horse, too."

Mentally apologizing to Zachariah for losing not only the saddlebags, but his horse, Nate surrendered the animal. "I did my part," Nate said as Mel mounted. "Now do yours."

But Mel rode off.

"Where's Hattie?" Nate cried out, despite being stranded.

31

Nate wanted to curse at Josephine. Then, he stopped short. He had an idea. But he had to keep his head in order to use his wits. "You've got your money. Now where's Hattie?" he called out again. "*Miss* Krugar?"

It took a moment, but a figure on horseback rode up to the rim of the ravine. She pulled off the hat, and blonde hair tied with a ribbon tumbled over her shoulder.

Nate grinned. When a man who has outsmarted everyone discovers someone's outsmarted him, he's got to know how. But curiosity of this nature wasn't solely a man's. It belonged to the arrogantly intelligent.

"How'd you know?" she asked.

"Let's just say we have a mutual acquaintance."

"And who might this 'mutual acquaintance' be?" She spoke with the diction of a woman who'd once enjoyed parties in the governor's mansion.

"You have no idea to whom I might be referring?"

"If I did, I wouldn't be asking you now, would I?" she said with a flirtatious flair.

Nate detected tightness in her voice. What part in all of this was Cadwell playing? How she responded to the *who* might give Nate a hint at the *what*. "Our mutual acquaintance," Nate said, "might be Jacob Cadwell."

"Jake?" She spoke the name too quickly, too

gently. "Where'd you make his acquaintance?" Though she played with words, there was no mistaking the way her back straightened. Josephine was in love with Cadwell.

"I'm afraid Cadwell's come and gone," Nate played her.

"Gone where?"

"I'm not sure where he went." Nate was happy to catch a glimpse of Clayton.

"Then tell me," she said. "Where'd you meet up with him?"

This ought to be good. "Church."

A pause. "I don't appreciate your humor."

He snickered.

Zachariah waved from behind a rock.

Nate shook his head slightly, signaling Zachariah to stay put until he knew where Hattie was. He offered Josephine a reason for the gesture. "My apologies, but I wasn't joking. So how about you and I stop talking about Cadwell and get back to business?"

"Yes, Nate. How about you and I get back to business."

"How'd you know my name?" Hattie wouldn't have mentioned him, would she?

"Let's just say we have another mutual acquaintance," she said, playing him now. "Small world, isn't it?"

No, the world was large. It was cold-hearted outlaws like her who made it feel crowded. "I suppose it is—Josephine."

"So we're on a first name basis now. How charming you are, my dear. My pretty guest here—"

Here? That meant Hattie was up there with her.

"—and I had a heart-to-heart talk. You hurt her,

Nate, but she still loves you. She said you wouldn't come."

That slashed Nate's heart.

"But I knew you would. And from what I can see from up here, you're more handsome than I'd thought you'd be. Rich would have suited me fine, but lucky little Pearl gets a rich, good-looking man to fall in love with her. I hope she appreciates you as much as I'm admiring you right now." Josephine crossed her arms. Was she smiling at him? "Just think," she continued. "With a little twist in fate, maybe I might have ended up the lucky one."

"Instead of ending up with Cadwell?"

She didn't answer, which meant that Nate had thrown the knife right back and hit his target.

A man appeared on the rim beside her.

"Well, Nate," Josephine said, "I enjoyed our little chat, but it's time to bid our farewells." She threw him a kiss and then turned her horse around to show that Hattie had been lying unconscious behind her.

Mel pulled Hattie off Josephine's horse, and her limp body hit the ground.

Nate lost his senses. "You're a poor excuse for a woman, Krugar!"

~*~

Nate? Hattie squinted from the sun. Was that Nate's voice she was hearing? She tried to sit up, but her body felt as if a stampede had gone over her. And her leg…she bit back the pain.

"Let's get out of here."

Josephine's smooth but treacherous voice and a shuffling of horses' feet brought back to Hattie that she was being swapped out for an impossible ten thousand dollars. *So why am I still alive? And why did I hear Nate?* A strange tang hit her nose. *And—why do I smell vinegar?*

She wasn't the only one who smelled it.

"Wait a minute." Josephine sniffed the air. "Mel, what's that odor?"

"It's the man from down yonder that smells. He spilled vinegar all over his clothes."

"If he's way down there, then why can I smell him from here?" Her eyes grew wide. "Where's the money?"

"In my saddlebag."

She opened it. "You imbecile."

~*~

Josephine had discovered the money was fake.

"Zachariah," Nate called out. "They're coming out from the ridge where you can see Skull Rock." Would Zachariah remember?

Hattie did. She crawled to the rim and looked down into the ravine. "Nate?"

Hattie. The sight of her took away his voice. She was bleeding, ragged. He cleared the lump in his throat. "Stay right where you are, Hattie. I'm coming." He ensured the gun was stuffed securely in his belt.

He managed to climb about three-quarters of the way up when his foothold crumbled beneath him. The rock broke loose and tumbled fifty feet down the incline. He hung onto a ridge barely wide enough for his two hands, his feet dangling.

From across the ravine, Clayton fired, and someone fired back, with Nate hanging by his fingertips in the crossfire. His legs flailed for a foothold and then he swung himself into a hollow.

Clayton continued to fire, while Zachariah aimed from another location. Zachariah fired, and the bullet hit the man in the shoulder, taking him out. It was good teamwork.

"There's another man out yonder!" Zachariah had been discovered.

The man with Josephine fired at Zachariah, making Zachariah duck.

Nate couldn't shoot because he needed to hold on with both hands to keep from falling. Where was Cadwell? He'd surely give them the advantage. Or, if Cadwell and Josephine were in love, give them the extreme disadvantage. Was he even here? Whose side was he on? The man was a mystery. But since Nate could see everything that was going on, he could help out. "Zachariah," he called. "There's a man by…" Could he say it? "…Sally's Ledge."

The place where Zachariah had carved Sally's name into the rock long ago.

A few minutes later, Zachariah came up from behind Mel, surprising him. Mel dropped his gun.

Nate heaved himself onto the next ridge. Eight feet from the top, a bullet chipped the rock above his head. He was in someone's sights. *Cadwell, I could use you right about now.* There was still no sign of him.

But then, there was no sign of Josephine, either.

Zachariah came through. He fired at the miscreant, missed, and rather than taking time to reload, threw the rifle down and snatched a revolver. He and Clayton hammered away at the man.

Nate pulled himself over the rim—and made it to Hattie.

She was breathing but barely moving. He covered her body with his to protect her from any stray bullets.

The shooting stopped.

"We got three of them, Nate," Zachariah called out. "Any idea where the last one might be?"

Long gone with Cadwell would have been Nate's best guess. He walked to the edge and found Clayton tying hands behind backs and Zachariah looking back at Nate. "No," Nate said. "But I've got Hattie."

"How is she?" Zachariah said.

"Not so good." He remembered six-year-old Hattie Brown shoved to the school ground, her knee bleeding, her dress dirty. She'd always be that little girl to him. How Cadwell could have fallen for that harpy was beyond Nate's comprehension. After what Josephine had done to Hattie, Nate wished he could dole out justice to her. He'd never hit a woman before, but he'd make an exception. When he turned back to Hattie, her eyes were wide with fear.

A shove from a rifle barrel nudged her head forward. "You tried to trick the wrong person, Nate," Josephine said.

32

Nate followed the length of a rifle from Hattie's blood-matted hair up to the stony expression of a cold-blooded murderer. His fingers tingled to grab the gun tucked in his belt, but he feared that by the time he drew, Hattie would have a bullet through her skull.

Zachariah and Clayton couldn't see what was going on up here. They were likely leaving to bring their prisoners back to Ramsden... or on their way to get Doc. Nate was on his own. Unless...

Cadwell was nowhere in sight. The man was a wildcard.

Nate didn't like not knowing whose side he was on or if he would decide to show up at the last minute. Hattie's life was in Nate's hands.

"Let her go," Nate said to Josephine. She was nothing more to him than Joe Krugar, the cold-blooded outlaw he'd seen in the shadows that night, who'd ordered the killing of an innocent man. "If you've got to kill someone so you can have the last word, shoot me."

"You're too handsome to kill, Nate."

"But she's beautiful," he said. "Inside and out."

With ice for eyes, Josephine looked down at the ragged form strewn at her feet. Josephine was nothing more than an ogress getting some sort of twisted joy out of crushing a fairy princess.

Hattie feebly looked up at Nate, and he wanted to

gather her in his arms and cry in her blood-matted hair. But he held up his hands hoping he could talk Josephine into turning her rifle on him. If he succeeded, his last game of wits would win him a bullet. "Let's talk about Jacob Cadwell," Nate said. "What did he do to you? Betray you? Abandon you? Did he fail to love you the way you needed him to?"

Josephine's eyes became distant. Her silence said that Nate was right. Cadwell had failed her in all these ways. Otherwise Cadwell would have been with her now.

"Don't take this out on Hattie. She doesn't deserve this," Nate said. "If you've got to hate someone, hate me. Because I did all these things to her."

"There is something special about our Pearl, isn't there?"

Nate's eyes glazed as he looked at Hattie. *Pearl.* Yes, that's exactly what she was.

"Even though she's a simple sort," Josephine said, "you can't deny there's something noble about her. I know she wouldn't have done to you what you did to her."

Was Josephine seeing in Hattie a little of the woman she'd once been? Nate hoped so. He smiled when Josephine lifted her rifle from Hattie and pointed it toward him. For the last time, he looked down at Hattie.

Her hair and forehead were caked with blood. Her leg jetted at an unnatural angle. Tears streaked her face as she whimpered, "Nate, don't do this."

He could barely see her through the glaze covering his eyes. If there was a last sight he wanted to take with him into the next world, she would be it. Just not like this. Because this, he realized, is what he'd done to her heart. "Go ahead. Kill me," he urged Josephine as he gazed at Hattie.

Josephine's eyes turned to steel. A shot rang out.

But it wasn't from Josephine's rifle.

Her hair tumbled down, the ribbon having been shot off. As she clutched where the ribbon had been, the cold calm in her eyes gave way to wide-eyed shock. She turned, looking for something in the rocky rim.

Cadwell stepped out and touched the rim of his hat to her.

"Jake." There was a softening in her voice and eyes as she gazed at Cadwell for one vulnerable moment.

Nate drew his gun on Josephine.

Cadwell shot the gun out of Nate's hand.

Josephine threw herself onto her horse, and hooves kicked up earth as she took off in a fury.

Nate looked to Cadwell, still standing on the rim. Why was he letting that killer get away? As though he was reading Nate's mind, Cadwell shook his head and then disappeared in a different direction.

The wildcard had been played. It had been in both Nate's and Josephine's hands.

33

On his knees by Hattie's side, Nate tore his shirt into bandages. He now had a fuller understanding of Hattie. She gave all of herself out of the goodness of her heart.

Zachariah thundered up on horseback. "What's going on? I heard more gunfire."

"That was Josephine." Nate bandaged the gash on Hattie's head. "You won't catch up to her."

Hattie lying on the ground, her hair and face crusted with blood, brought Zachariah down from his horse. "I'm sorry, Hattie. Nate was right. I never should have let you do this." Zachariah fell to his knees, and she reached for him to hold her. Zachariah gathered her into his arms, and it was the first time Nate had ever seen her cry. But he knew by the way she sobbed into Zachariah's shoulder that this wasn't the first time Zachariah had seen her cry.

Nate hung his head. No, she'd never cried on his shoulder. It was always him doing the crying and her doing the comforting. He'd always thought she was unbreakable. How self-centered he'd been. He felt no jealousy toward the brotherly way Zachariah caressed her, rocked her. Zachariah was good for her. No wonder she couldn't leave him.

Her sobs calmed.

"You don't look so good, Hattie," Zachariah said.

She spoke between a groan and a chuckle, "I don't

feel so good, either."

"How about I bring you over to Doc's?"

"I sure would appreciate it."

She looked like a worn-out rag doll as Zachariah lifted her up.

Nate carefully took her from Zachariah, so Zachariah could get on his horse.

Hattie leaned her head against Nate's chest. She felt fragile in his arms. She looked at him. "Jesus, please help Nate find his way to forgiving Zachariah," she whispered.

Nate handed her up to Zachariah.

"You've got no horse, Nate," Zachariah said. "I'll send someone back for you."

"Don't worry about me." Nate said. "It's a nice day for a walk." Watching Zachariah ride away with Hattie stirred some long-forgotten memories.

~*~

"Look at you with that wavy yellow hair." The woman who cleaned his room at the asylum had said to Nate as he lay in bed. He didn't mind her so much anymore. "You sure are one handsome child of God. I bet you've broken plenty of hearts with those light blue eyes of yours."

Nate looked far away through the window where the drapes rippled with the breeze and the sun shone through. "Only the heart that mattered," he said.

"So you did have a sweetheart." The cleaning woman smiled as she mopped. "The woman who won your heart must have been beautiful."

"She was the Song of Solomon," Nate said, staring out the window. "I'll never forgive myself for the way I treated her."

"I don't think anybody who's really sorry for what they've done can forgive themselves," the woman said as she swished the mop. "So that's what I suppose Jesus is all about."

He chuckled lightly. He was getting used to her. "You're not preaching at me, are you?"

She held up her mop. "Do I look like a preacher, Nathan? I keep telling you. I'm just the cleaning woman."

No. She was more than just a cleaning woman.

"I killed my sister."

Now able to get out of bed by himself, Nate sat in the chair and stared out his window. The sky was overcast and raindrops tapped the glass.

"You killed Sally? On purpose?" The cleaning woman put a hand on her hip. "I don't believe that one bit. You loved her too much."

Nate watched as beads of raindrops filled the window. "She died because I was jealous." He hung his head, and the cleaning lady set aside her mop and came to his side. She held him as he wept.

"You dear, dear child of God. Do you know what I think jealousy is?"

Leaning against her, he shook his head.

"I think jealousy is just plain not loving yourself."

"I thought your Good Book said that you're not supposed to love yourself."

"It says not to think of yourself more highly than you ought to. But you ought to think something of yourself. How can you love your neighbor as much as yourself, if you hate yourself? Imagine that. What kind of a neighbor would you be then, fighting all the time like vermin? You're created in the image of God, child. Not a lousy rat. The Good Book ain't about hating yourself, Nathan. It's a love letter from God to anybody on earth who wants to read it, and that includes *you. Unless you think you're from the moon. But that would make you a crazy person now, wouldn't it?"*

In the end, it wasn't the doctor who'd healed Nate. It was the cleaning woman.

Nate sat on the edge of his bed, dressed in traveling clothes. He could have left four hours earlier, but there was someone he wanted to say good-bye to first.

The cleaning woman walked in with her mop, eyed him, and then her dark face broadened with a smile. "I sure am going to miss you, Nathan." She set her mop in a corner and sat on the bed beside him. "Where're you headed to?"

"Cambridge, Massachusetts. I have a year left of college, and I'll finish my degree. After that, I'll get a good job and buy a big house, and then…" He looked out his window one last time. It was a clear, sunny day. "And then, I'm going back for her."

She patted his hand. "Good for you, Nathan." She reached into a deep apron pocket. "There's something I want to give you before you go." She pulled out a Bible with a worn spine.

There was a time he would have thrown it back at her. He accepted her gift, but not without a comment. "I'm not exactly the 'child of God' you keep saying I am."

"Oh, yes, you are. And someday you'll figure that out."

"I doubt it."

"I don't, because I pray for you every single day, dear Nathan, and I'll keep on praying for you until the day I die."

He shook his head and then came to his feet. "Is there a name I can remember 'the woman who prays for me' by?"

"You can remember me by the name of Hattie."

He cocked his head. "Hattie?"

"Yes. That's my name. Hattie."

He snorted. "That's a coincidence, because the woman I'm going back for just happens to have the same name."

"Why, that is a coincidence." She winked at him. "So I guess that means you'll have to invite me to the wedding."

He solemnly made her a promise. "If by some miracle she says yes to my proposal, I will personally pay for your train ticket to our wedding. You brought me back—Hattie."

He fell on her shoulder, and as they hugged good-bye, she said, "No, Nathan, it was the Lord who brought you back. And He's got some unfinished business for you to do."

~*~

Nate's walk ended with him in Ramsden, standing in front of that unfinished business.

~*~

The dose of laudanum Doc gave Hattie left a bitter taste in her mouth and was just beginning to kick in as he finished the last stinging stitch on her head. She wasn't sure if she was glad he'd waited a mite longer before yanking her leg back where it belonged, because although the laudanum numbed her grit, the howl she let out was loud enough to wake the dead.

After the patching up, which seemed worse than the infliction, was over, Prudence, Doc's wife, bathed Hattie and slipped her into a clean nightdress. They moved her to a bedroom where the walls were papered with flowers and the bed sheets were soft and smelled of lavender.

Prudence placed a soft hand on Hattie's shoulder. "It'll take some time for you to heal, but I've seen worse. In the meantime, you're staying here where I can keep an eye on you."

Hattie's eyelids started getting heavy. "What

about my pies?"

"Kate won't go out of business if she's without them for a while."

"What about my chickens?"

"We'll take care of them."

"What about—"

"We'll take care of everything, Hattie. You need to stop worrying and start healing."

"You can talk to her now," Doc said to someone outside the bedroom door. "But don't take too long with her. She needs to rest."

Prudence left to allow that someone some time alone with Hattie.

Zachariah entered.

Hattie eyed the way he reverently held his hat in front of him. "You don't have to hold on to your hat like that, Zachariah. I'm in a bed, not a coffin." Though if worse did come to worst, she didn't have far to go. She looked out the window at the graveyard. Funny how it was right next door to Doc's.

Actually, it wasn't so funny.

Zachariah got rid of the hat by placing it on the dresser. "You came close, Hattie. Too close."

"And I've got you and Nate to thank for saving my life."

"You've got that half right. You've got me to thank for getting you into this mess."

"As you recall, distracting the gang was all my idea."

"And I shouldn't have let you do it."

"So you'd have done it instead? Strut around in the dress?" She smiled a crooked smile and then giggled at the image.

Zachariah picked up the bottle of laudanum on the

bedside table. "How much of this did Doc give you?"

"A couple spoonfuls."

Zachariah arched a brow.

She was talking silly, and she didn't care. "You know what, Zachariah?" She snuggled into her pillow. It was soft and cool and smelled so heavenly nice.

"What Hattie?"

"This ain't the first time you and Nate teamed up to rescue me, you know." She gasped. "Did I say *ain't*?" She snickered. "I ain't said *ain't* in years. I'd given it up to impress the Reverend, who never impressed me, but you know what, Zachariah? It sure feels good to say it again. Ain't." She let out a laugh.

Zachariah shook his head.

"You and Nate rescuing me. It happened on the school grounds. I was six years old." She yawned, and the thoughts continued, though she wasn't sure if she was talking about it or dreaming about it. Just that it was a bad memory that had somehow turned to a good one. One of the boys had shoved her, and she landed in the mud. It wasn't because of all the scrubbing she'd have to put into getting her dress clean that made her eyes glaze over, it was what the children who'd gathered around her were saying.

~*~

Hattie ain't got no pa.
That's why she and her ma
don't go to church,
'cause God would lurch
And strike them both down dead.

"Leave her alone!" One of the older boys barged into the ring. She knew he didn't have a pa, either, but for some *reason, folks took to caring for his widowed ma.*

The boy who'd knocked her down challenged, "What are you going to do, Zachariah?"

"Whatever it takes to get you to leave that girl alone."

"You can't take on all five of us."

"No." Zachariah rolled up his sleeves. "But those I can take on, I reckon I can wallop good."

A second boy stepped into the ring. He was light-haired with serious blue eyes in a face so pleasant it was hard to stop looking at him.

"And I can take on the rest of you," he said.

She later came to call them the undefeatable team of Nate Powell and Zachariah Keene. They were the best of friends and were apt to step in for those who couldn't stand up for themselves. Together they'd put down many a fight without raising a fist, because Zachariah was the tallest and brawniest boy in school, and for those not scared off by his size, there was Nate.

No one argued with Nate Powell. Not when he could outsmart them all.

~*~

Hattie was feeling melancholy. "Why'd he have to come back, Zachariah? Why couldn't Nate have just stayed away?"

"I reckon he hoped he'd make you fall in love with him again," Zachariah said with tenderness.

"Doesn't he realize I never stopped loving him?"

Zachariah crossed his arms and stared out the window. Whatever had gotten his interest was nothing she could fathom. There was nothing out there but sunset and headstones. He sighed and then kissed her on the forehead. "You rest up now, Hattie."

34

Nate read the name inscribed on the headstone before him. *I don't know if I can do this.* He shifted his weight as he looked up toward where the sun was getting low in the sky and a swatch of clouds took on a purplish hue.

Even though he'd lost Hattie, maybe the cleaning woman was right. Maybe he'd come back for something else. Maybe he did have some unfinished business here in Ramsden. A breeze blew through his hair as he looked back down at the name MARCUS POWELL.

Where to begin?

He'd start with a deep breath. "I didn't know that you had died. I was in no state of mind to receive that news. As a matter of fact, if someone had told me about your passing a month ago, I would have come back just to spit on your grave."

He stepped closer. "I don't know why I'm not spitting on it now. You sent me to an asylum where the doctor was crazier than the patients. Do you know what they did to me? They gave up on me. Just like you did. I came out of my melancholy because of a cleaning woman. That's right. A woman who came into my room and dusted the window sills and mopped the floor. She came in day after day, and she cared enough about me to talk to me while she worked." His voice cracked. "She was the only visitor I ever had." He tried to clear his throat, but it was an ache lodged deeper, like a jackknife in his heart. "Do you know that I don't have it in me to call you father?

"Marcus. That's all you are to me. Marcus Powell, the boss man. Marcus Powell, the rich man. Marcus Powell, the man who thought he knew everything because he'd worked his way from a cowhand to the most successful rancher in the county. But now that death has shut your mouth for good, let me tell you a thing or two, beginning with the fact that all your money is gone. Your home is gone. You left Mother destitute and at the mercy of a hard-nosed banker. But don't worry about her, because I made sure she'll be well provided for. Because everything you've worked your entire life for is gone. Your business failed. It's as dead as you are.

"And let me tell you something else, Mr. 'I Know Everything.' You didn't even know your own son. Do you know that I haven't read a poem since the day you took my book away? The teacher chose *me* to teach school because she thought I was *intelligent*. I read poetry because I *understood* it." His voice tightened. "Didn't that mean anything to you? Because it meant the world to me. I was honored. I was proud of myself. I thought you would be also." He spewed, "You hurt me deeply, Pa."

Had he said Pa?

He fell to his knees in the scraggly grass in front of the headstone. "All I ever wanted was for you to brag on me as much as you did Zachariah. All I ever wanted was for you to see what I could do." He held his hands to his chest for a moment and then dropped them.

"Maybe you had the wrong son all along. Maybe Zachariah should have been born to you instead. A natural cowboy. That's what you wanted, wasn't it? But it was never who I was. You tried to force me to drive cattle and then settled for making me an accountant for your business. I guess you figured working with books was good enough for me. You sent me to school for it. I quit. You pressed me to go back. Then things got even crazier." He looked into the purple and then back at the name.

"Well, I'm back from earning my accounting degree. You were right in the sense it turned out to be a good way to make a living. As a matter of fact, I'm the vice president of a bank. I wear a suit and tie to work; I have men twice my age calling me 'Sir.' You'd be amazed at the house I live in. It's three stories high, and there are two maples taller than the roof. Their leaves turn red in autumn, and they bow like two giant doormen over the front stairs. The house has a foyer with a chandelier, and the banister along the stairs is made of cherry wood so smooth it's like running your hand over warm ice. I have a kitchen fit for a chef, a dining room grand enough to hold a dinner party for the governor, two parlors, ten bedrooms, and–" He abruptly looked down. "And there's no one to share it with.

"Wealth without love is loneliness, and loneliness is the worst kind of poverty. So what good is boasting about a fine house that only makes me feel like a pauper? And worse, bragging about it to someone who's dead? You're dead, Pa." A sob escaped him. "Guess you thought cowboying was the only way to make a living out here, and out here was the only place to live. I thought I was a city man. But now I know why you loved Ramsden.

"And I know why you appreciated Zachariah. You

knew about Sally all along, didn't you? That it was me who'd slacked off on his responsibility, and she fired up the stove so I wouldn't get the switch. I saw the smoke. I just couldn't get to her in time. I held her in my arms, Pa. I held my little sister in my arms, and there was nothing left to her but char and blisters. All her hair had been burned off, and when I looked into her face–"

Nate wiped his eyes. "So I guess that's what made Zachariah your son. If things hadn't gone the way they did, he'd have been your son-in-law, because Sally loved him. And so does Hattie, just in a different way. She loves him the same way you did, I suppose. Come to think of it, the way I did once." Nate smiled at the long-ago memory of playing hide-and-seek in the ravine with Zachariah. "I can't blame you for taking to him the way you did. He's a good man. There's a lot about him to respect. But I'm trying, Pa. I'm trying hard to be a better man, too."

His sobs came out unrestrained. "I'm sorry for blaming Zachariah for Sally's death. I'm sorry for all the times I mocked you, Pa. I never thought you were stupid, I just wanted you to see that my strength wasn't in my arms, it was in my head. I wanted you to be just as proud of me as you were of Zachariah but in the ways that were my own." He fell on the headstone and cried himself out.

A hand came to rest on his shoulder. "Hattie wouldn't be alive were it not for you. Good plan, Nate."

Nate came to his feet but held his gaze away from Zachariah and onto the darkening sky. "You did some fine shooting, Zachariah. You saved my neck today."

"I figured I had a minute or two to spare, so why

not?"

Nate smiled. Zachariah had always been a banterer.

"We made a great team out there today," Zachariah said.

Nate nodded. It was strange talking with Zachariah again, instead of at him. "How's Hattie doing?"

"She's at Doc's, resting. She's got a broken leg, some cracked ribs, a concussion, but she'll make it. Be a while before she's on her feet again. She's not as mad at me as she ought to be. As for you—" Zachariah looked at the nearby house where one window glowed and the vegetable garden outside had become shapes in the dusk. "—She ain't never going to be happy without you."

That made two of them. Nate sidestepped the subject. "I saw that you and Clayton got three of the gang."

"Yup. Got them locked up."

"It's too bad we didn't get Joe Krugar." Nate's was an understatement. All on account of Cadwell being weak for a woman. Maybe Nate had an inkling of what it felt like to forever be in love; however, the object of Cadwell's affection, that ogress who hurt Hattie, was another story. But it was a story Nate would keep secret.

"The important thing is, we got Hattie back," Zachariah said. "I should have listened to you in the first place and never let her do it, Nate."

"And tell headstrong Hattie what to do?" Zachariah's hand felt warm and friendly on Nate's shoulder. "Do you really think she would have listened to you?"

Zachariah offered back a grin that needed a shave. His scar didn't look so ugly. Then Zachariah sighed. "What happened to us, Nate? We were best of friends once. Why, we could stand against anything. I remember back when some boys were picking on Hattie, and we were willing to take on all four of them."

Nate thought back on that day in the schoolyard. "It was five boys," he corrected.

Zachariah frowned. "Whose big idea was it to take on five?"

"Yours."

Zachariah rubbed his jaw. "It was a good thing nobody called our bluff. We'd have gotten whopped good."

Both men laughed at their childish fortitude.

"So why can't we overcome what stands between us now?" Zachariah asked. "I remembered spitting in our hands and clasping them in a vow that even death wouldn't separate us."

Nate remembered too well. "Sally's death happened, and I blamed you." He shook his head. "Why didn't you defend yourself? Why didn't you tell the judge it was all my fault? Why did you let everyone believe—"

"Because you loved your sister, and I loved my friend. I saw what was going on between you and your pa. I didn't like the way he favored me over you, but I didn't know how to be less than I was."

Nate had never considered that Zachariah had lost both parents by the time he'd turned eleven, and life required him to become a man instead of a boy. "Life must have been hard on you."

"I think life's taken its toll on the both of us, Nate."

"So is that what's come between us?" Nate asked. "Life?"

"I reckon so."

"Then let's make another vow," Nate said, "that life won't come between us, either." He spat on his hand and offered it to Zachariah. As they shook hands, Nate fell on Zachariah's shoulder. "Forgive me, my friend."

~*~

Hattie lay in bed, her mind in a dreamy mist as she looked out the window at something more beautiful than the lavender sunset. Her eyelids were heavy as anvils, but every time they dropped, she pulled them back open. Though they were getting heavier, she didn't want them to shut for fear the picture of Zachariah and Nate hugging one another would disappear forever.

Prudence came in and scolded, "You've got a lot of healing to do. You're supposed to be resting and letting the laudanum do its work." She drew the drapes shut and tucked in Hattie's bed sheets, which she'd already tucked in perfectly before. She kissed Hattie on the forehead and whispered, "Sweet dreams, Hattie."

"Yes, Prudence." Hattie's eyelids drifted shut, and she tugged at them but could no longer pull them open. "I just had the sweetest dream I've ever...ever...had."

35

Hattie leaned toward Nate. "I love you," she whispered, "and I always will."

"I love you too, Hattie," Nate whispered back. "In a whole new way now."

Hattie couldn't keep her eyes off Nate in a black cutaway coat, wing tip collar and tie, and a yellow boutonniere.

His gaze didn't budge from her either. But then again, she'd never felt more beautiful wearing the ivory satin wedding dress he'd bought her. The skirt was layers of lace, and the veil was silk tulle trimmed with pearls so that she felt like a jewel. She had a dozen yellow roses in her bouquet. A beam of morning sunlight smiled in on them from the east windows of the church, and a fresh breeze poured in from the west, making it the most perfect day ever.

However, the wedding had hit a lull due to a not-so-unpredictable glitch.

Reverend Everton, who was presiding over the ceremony, had gotten into a pickle when his "Dearly beloved" had been interrupted with a *plop*.

"But if two imperfect people get together," Hattie whispered during that lull, "doesn't that make things twice as bad?"

"Negative one plus negative one equals negative two." Nate frowned. "It's an accounting disaster, and I'd advise any stockholder against it."

With butterfingers, the Reverend was still fishing his eyeglasses out of his glass of water while two deacons scrambled on all fours mopping up the puddles with their handkerchiefs so the Reverend wouldn't slip. But for every drop they sopped up, he spilled two. Nate stepped in closer to Hattie to allow one deacon to scurry by and catch another spill. Meanwhile, the men in the pews were wide-eyed and the women held hands over hearts in hopes that the Reverend wouldn't trip over the deacons. Hattie, however, wasn't worried one bit, because she knew the Reverend's secret.

"Still think he's a deadeye?" she whispered to Nate.

Nate smiled as the Reverend splashed, groping for his eyeglasses. "I don't know what got into me."

The Reverend's secret was that it took not only two deacons but also a dozen harried angels to keep him from a catastrophe. Heaven only knew what would have befallen the poor fellow had God not sent help.

"I always wanted a righteous man," she whispered. "I'm sure glad it turned out to be you."

The Reverend retrieved his glasses and put them on his nose, but there was another delay as one of the deacons took them off, wiped the droplets off the lenses, and put them back on the Reverend. Then one deacon refilled the water glass, offered it to the Reverend, and while the Reverend took a sip, the other deacon took charge of the Reverend's eyeglasses by standing behind and holding them in place. The first deacon received the water glass back, and with a drink successfully accomplished, the ceremony continued until the Reverend asked of best man, Zachariah, "Do you have the ring?"

Zachariah handed the ring to Nate. And then there was another hiccup. But this time, it wasn't the Reverend's doing.

Nate dropped the ring.

Hattie gasped.

Jaws fell as everyone in the pews gasped.

Did courting Hattie turn a man into a stumblebum?

Nate plucked the ring off the floor. "I hear it's a blessing to drop the ring during the ceremony. It's supposed to shake out all the bad things that could happen."

Instead of appreciating the irony, Hattie set a hand on her hip. "If you ever do anything like that to me again, Mr. Nate Powell..." His wink softened her heart. "So if the numbers say that you and I equal disaster," she said, "how will we make this work as a couple?"

"By making a couple three," he said. "We both have Jesus in our lives now."

Nate slipped the ring on her finger, and the Reverend put the frosting on the cake by announcing, "I now pronounce you man and wife."

The kiss that followed was so sweet and tender, Hattie wanted it to go on forever. Nate promised he'd continue the kiss that night, and she bound him to it.

Everyone stood and applauded, although Hattie wasn't sure if it was to congratulate her and Nate or to express relief that the ceremony was completed without further disaster.

Outside, the church grounds had been set up with tents and tables, each with a white tablecloth and a centerpiece of roses. The food came from Kate's, including a cake five tiers high, and Kate and the chef

Nate brought in from Boston cooked up a tender roast beef and topped it with a sauce Hattie couldn't pronounce but had no trouble savoring. Nate had hired a band from Kansas City to complete the grandest party Ramsden had ever seen.

While people were dancing, Nate's mother hugged Hattie. "Thank you for making him stay," Mother Powell said.

Then Nate tugged Hattie away. "There's someone special I'd like you to meet." He brought her over to a woman sitting with Hattie's father, who had walked her up the aisle during the ceremony.

The woman came to her feet and clasped Hattie's hand between two brown hands. "Why Nathan, so this is the woman you came back for. No wonder. She's as beautiful as you said she was. I waited for your invitation, you know. I waited for it because I knew you would get married. I prayed for it every single day."

Hattie's father came to his feet and said to Hattie, "You have no idea who this lovely lady is, do you?"

Nate had told her about a cleaning woman at the asylum who'd helped him, but Hattie answered more discretely, "She's a dear friend of Nate's from back East."

"A dear friend of Nate's, you say." Hattie's father chuckled. "Indeed, this lady is even more dear to you. Why, this is Henrietta Brown."

Hattie touched her chest. "But that's my name." Then it occurred to her that this woman was her aunt. "My mother's sister?"

Henrietta was just as surprised. "My sister's little girl?"

They fell into each other's arms.

~*~

Nate stepped back. Watching two special women cry happy tears was like seeing the square of a miracle. He walked back into the church and his eyes glistened with pure joy as he looked up at a coarse wooden cross. It was learning to see himself through Christ's eyes, and not Marcus's, that had fixed everything.

Cadwell came up from behind. "You've got yourself a good woman, Nate."

"As a matter of fact, I do," Nate said. "Love can be a good pair of eyeglasses making you see things clearer, or it can be a blindfold."

Cadwell paused. "I see you figured out my weakness."

"It was obvious when you let Josephine escape."

"You know." Cadwell looked at his shoes. "This wasn't the first time I've let her get away from me."

"Who are you exactly?" Nate asked. "A bounty hunter gone soft?"

"More like a U.S. Marshal gone soft. Which, by the way, is why you saw me in the 'Wanted' poster. I was infiltrating the gang. Josephine's a woman on the run with good reason."

"Care to elaborate on what that reason is?"

"That information is classified 'Top Secret' by the U.S. Government." He looked out the window. "So I'll be sticking around Ramsden for a while longer. She knows where I am now. She'll be back. There's some good in her, Nate. I know there is."

After what she'd done to Hattie, Nate figured it would take a miracle for Cadwell to find the good in her, or to figure out that there wasn't any. Either way,

Nate had some advice to offer. "In the meantime, if you need to wear a disguise again, you might want to consider..."

Cadwell smirked. "Something less lacy?"

"Or at least something that matches your hat."

"I will take that under consideration," Cadwell said.

"Oh, and one more thing." Nate paused. "Are Hattie and I really married, or do I have to rely on Common Law?"

Cadwell put a steady hand on Nate's shoulder. "You can enjoy your wedding night fully assured that I am indeed an ordained minister."

Nate and Cadwell walked outside where Nate rejoined Hattie, and, with a well-timed stumble, Cadwell turned back into Reverend Everton.

Zachariah shook Nate's hand and kissed Hattie on the cheek. "Congratulations to the both of you. And congratulations to you, Nate, on the new job. A lot of people in this town will be happy to put Tilly out of business."

When Nate had called the bank to tell them he was quitting, they decided to build a bank in Ramsden. Apparently, Nate was very good at what he did.

He held Hattie by the waist and pulled her closer. "Thank you, Zachariah. I'm hoping to make a difference in this town."

"It looks like you already have." With a pat on the back, Zachariah left, and the cleaning lady squeezed between Nate and Hattie and held each by the hand.

"I can't tell you how happy I am for the two of you. My dear Nathan. My little sister's baby girl." Her eyes sparkled. "Who but the Lord could have done that."

Thank you

We appreciate you reading this White Rose Publishing title. For other inspirational stories, please visit our on-line bookstore at www.pelicanbookgroup.com.

For questions or more information, contact us at customer@pelicanbookgroup.com.

White Rose Publishing
Where Faith is the Cornerstone of Love™
an imprint of Pelican Book Group
www.PelicanBookGroup.com

Connect with Us
www.facebook.com/Pelicanbookgroup
www.twitter.com/pelicanbookgrp

To receive news and specials, subscribe to our bulletin
http://pelink.us/bulletin

May God's glory shine through
this inspirational work of fiction.

AMDG

You Can Help!

At Pelican Book Group it is our mission to entertain readers with fiction that uplifts the Gospel. It is our privilege to spend time with you awhile as you read our stories.

We believe you can help us to bring Christ into the lives of people across the globe. And you don't have to open your wallet or even leave your house!

Here are 3 simple things you can do to help us bring illuminating fiction™ to people everywhere.

1) If you enjoyed this book, write a positive review. Post it at online retailers and websites where readers gather. And share your review with us at reviews@pelicanbookgroup.com (this does give us permission to reprint your review in whole or in part.)

2) If you enjoyed this book, recommend it to a friend in person, at a book club or on social media.

3) If you have suggestions on how we can improve or expand our selection, let us know. We value your opinion. Use the contact form on our web site or e-mail us at customer@pelicanbookgroup.com

God Can Help!

Are you in need? The Almighty can do great things for you. Holy is His Name! He has mercy in every generation. He can lift up the lowly and accomplish all things. Reach out today.

Do not fear: I am with you; do not be anxious: I am your God. I will strengthen you, I will help you, I will uphold you with my victorious right hand.
~Isaiah 41:10 (NAB)

We pray daily, and we especially pray for everyone connected to Pelican Book Group—that includes you! If you have a specific need, we welcome the opportunity to pray for you. Share your needs or praise reports at http://pelink.us/pray4us

Free Book Offer

We're looking for booklovers like you to partner with us! Join our team of influencers today and periodically receive free eBooks and exclusive offers.

For more information
Visit http://pelicanbookgroup.com/booklovers

www.ingramcontent.com/pod-product-compliance
Lightning Source LLC
Chambersburg PA
CBHW052040240626
47153CB00006B/2175